RETRIBUTION

RETRIBUTION

John Fulton

PICADOR USA

NEW YORK

Picador® is a U.S. registered trademark and is used by St. Martin's Press under license from Pan Books Limited.

www.picadorusa.com

Most of these stories have been published in periodicals and anthologies. "Braces" first appeared in *Zoetrope* (Fall 1999, vol. 3, no. 3) and was reprinted in Spanish translation in *Habra Una Vez,* an anthology of young North American writers. "Clean Away" was published in *Sonora Review* (Spring/Summer 1998). "Rose" was published in *The Southern Review* (Fall 1999, vol. 35, no. 4). "Iceland" was published in *The Florida Review* (Summer 1999, vol. 24, no. 2). "The Troubled Dog" won third prize in the 1997 *Playboy* College Fiction Contest. "Outlaws" originally appeared in *New York Stories* (Fall 1999) and was reprinted in *The Sun* (Winter 2001). "Visions" appeared in *Passages North* (Winter 2000). "First Sex" appeared in *Third Coast* (Spring 2001). "Liars" was published in *The American Literary Review* (Spring 2000).

Book design by Tim Hall

Library of Congress Cataloging-in-Publication Data

Fulton, John.
    Retribution and other stories / John Fulton.–1st ed.
        p.   cm.
    Contents: Braces–Clean away–Rose–Iceland–The troubled dog–Outlaws–Visions–First sex–Liars–Stealing–Retribution.
    ISBN 0-312-27680-X
    1. United States–Social life and customs–20th century–Fiction.   I. Title: Retribution.   II. Title.

PS3606.U58 R4 2001
813'.6–dc21

2001021931

First Edition: July 2001

10 9 8 7 6 5 4 3 2 1

To my parents

ACKNOWLEDGMENTS

This book would not have been possible without the help of many. I would like to thank my teachers and workshop at Michigan; Eric Gudas, Joshua Henkin, Paisley Rekdal, Christopher Shainan, and Ian Twiss, excellent friends and great readers; Jaunfer Merino, a true man of letters; Alicka Pistik, my agent; and most of all, Eve.

CONTENTS

RETRIBUTION

BRACES

That afternoon I had just gotten the last of my braces on and Mom had dropped me off at home, then left again, when Dad started calling. My mouth felt heavy and cramped with metal. I kept touching the wire with my tongue, trying to get used to the sharp, spiky feel of it. Dad called about every fifteen minutes and said, "Your mom home yet?" and I had to keep telling him no. Each time he called, he'd say, "So how are you, Mikey?" as if he hadn't talked to me two or three times already. He was a little loose, I could tell. He was the only one I let call me by Mikey anymore, because he'd been gone since early December—when Mom kicked him out of the house—and didn't know that I'd decided to go by Michael now.

"You're talking sort of funny," he said. I told him about the braces. "That's right," he said. "How they feel?"

"They hurt," I said. "I can't eat anything. But Mom says they're handsome. She says they do something for me."

"Good boy," he said. "Good boy." His voice sounded happy with me. Then his tone changed. "She's out, isn't she? She's with another guy, right?"

"No," I said. "She's getting her hair done or something." That was true, though later, after the hairdresser, she had plans to see Larry or Jim, both guys she'd been sort of dating recently.

Ben, my older sister's pet rat, climbed up the couch and started nibbling on my fingers. Ben was about the size of a kitten and Sarah had bought him because other kids in our school kept rats as pets. There was something hip in a disgusting, industrial way about owning one. He kept nibbling at my fingers—his way of saying he's hungry. I walked into the kitchen, with Ben scurrying in front of me. He knew he was going to be fed. Mom had bought a new cordless phone that you could walk anywhere with. I popped a bag of popcorn in the microwave and looked through the little window as it turned around on the carousel in that radioactive yellow light. I knew what Dad was going to say next. He'd been calling for the last four days, saying the same thing.

"Listen, Mikey," Dad said. "I don't want to put you in the middle of this, okay? But your mother needs to understand that the Mustang is mine. I owned that car before we married. I know she's hidden it. She's got it parked at one of her friends' or something. Will you please tell her I know that?"

"Sure," I said. The popcorn began popping and I felt Ben on the kitchen floor circling my leg, growing more excited because he recognized the sound of his favorite food.

"You know where it's parked, don't ya?" he said.

"No," I lied.

"Good boy," he said, really happy again. "Don't let yourself get caught in the middle of this, all right?"

"I won't," I said.

"All right," he said.

"All right," I said.

———

I opened the bag of popcorn and tried to eat a piece, but it hurt like hell because of the braces. So I put the bag down between my feet, where Ben could burrow into it and feed. Ben was a real pig when it came to popcorn, and he was eating so fast right now that the bag sort of spasmed between my feet.

When the phone rang next, it was Sarah. Sarah had taken off—she was a runaway, I guess—the day after Christmas with her boyfriend, Marcus. They ended up in San Francisco—a long way from Orem, Utah—living in this abandoned school building. Sarah had gone sort of crazy living at home with Mom and me. She renamed herself Nancy for no good reason, and you had to call her Nancy or she wouldn't answer you. Then she started speaking in a British accent and using British words like *bollocks* and *over the top* and *brilliant*. For her, everything was *brilliant—brilliant . . . brilliant . . . brilliant*—which was funny, because she'd never been to Britain. Mom started calling her "the foreigner." "Tell the foreigner that she's got to do those dishes," she'd say. The only time Sarah used her normal voice was when she spoke to Ben, which she did a lot, especially if Mom was around. Once, Mom told her to stop talking to that animal and to be herself. Sarah looked at her and said in her heavy British accent, "I'm sorry, Mummy, but I don't feel real with you."

The morning after Christmas, I woke up and found Ben scurrying around in the kitchen, hungry and dragging his leash behind him. (Sarah had kept him on a little leather leash, the way you'd keep a small dog.) There was this paper tag on Ben's collar that said:

Dear Mikey,
Sarah ran away and left me.
Please look after me, please!

So of course I did. What had Ben done to anyone? He just
ate and slept and lived. He had it all right, I guess. Besides,
he was a white rat, a fluffy, irresistible white like you would
expect a rabbit to be. He'd nudge at your hand for affection,
nudge away until you gave him some. He needed me, and
I liked that.

"Where's Mom, Mikey?" Sarah asked when I answered
the phone.

I said, "Michael, not Mikey, please."

"Oh, yeah," she said. "So where's Mom?"

"She's getting her hair done or something."

She asked why I was speaking like a dork and I told her
about the braces and she said, "Ouch. That hurts." It did—
my mouth felt tight and wooden and every word I said
hurt me. "At least no more buckteeth, right?" Then she
said, "Ching, ching. That costs money. Where's Mom getting the money for that?"

"You still living in the school building?" I asked.

"No," she said. "We bolted. It was too freaky sleeping in
a room with all those blackboards on the walls. I mean, I
was living in a school, and I always hated school so much."
Then she paused. "So where's Mom getting the money for
your mouth?"

"If you're not in the school building," I said, "where are
you?"

"I got to go," she said. "This is costing me."

I knew she was lying. Mom had somehow sent her one
of those "call home" calling cards so that Sarah could call
home on Mom.

"You got a number there you could give us?"

Outside, a light snow began to fall. The flakes were fine and ashy and the sky was this polluted gray color. She said, "I got to go, okay? You tell Mom I could use a little of that money, wherever it's coming from. Later, Mikey."

I said, "I talked to Dad just now. He called a minute ago."

"Oh," she said. She was going to stay on the line now. "He have much to say?"

"He was worried about his car."

"That stupid car," she said. "He was fucked up, wasn't he?"

"He was maybe a little loose," I said. I hated the way she had to use the worst words for everything.

"Did he ask about me?" The line beeped then—we had call waiting—and I told her that Dad was probably on the other line and to hold on, and she said, "All right, but this is costing me."

Dad said, "Your mother sold the fucking Mustang, didn't she?" He was almost shouting, his speech slushy and reckless, the way it got when he really let himself go. "I know she sold it. She sold it, didn't she, Mikey?"

I said, "No, she didn't sell it."

"But she's going to sell it. She's going to sell it, isn't she?"

I said, "Sarah's on the other line."

"Just tell me she's not going to sell the Mustang."

I told him that. Then I said, "Sarah's on the other line. She wants to know if you asked about her."

"So she's not going to sell it?"

"No," I said.

Then he said, "Your sister's not crying wolf again, is she? She's not saying she's in some hospital, is she?"

She'd done that a few times—called up and told Mom that she'd been in an accident and was in a hospital and needed an operation, then hung up without leaving a num-ber or the name of a hospital, so that Mom stayed up the whole night biting her nails bloody and calling around to different hospitals in the Bay Area, when Sarah wasn't in any of them.

"No," I said. "She's not crying wolf. She'd like to talk to you. Could she call you collect?"

"You know how I feel about that, Mikey. She chose to live out there on her own. She can pay for her own phone calls. I've got to go now, kid. Tell your mom that we need to talk."

"What's he say?" Sarah asked.

"He says to say hi. He says to ask what's up."

"What else?"

"He's sort of worried about his car. He thinks Mom's going to sell it." As soon as I said that, I knew I shouldn't have.

"She'd do that to him? She'd sell his car?" She was laughing.

"No," I said. "No, she wouldn't."

"Bullshit she wouldn't. That car's worth *mucho* buckage." Then she was quiet for a second. "That's how she's going to pay for your mouth, isn't it?"

"No," I said. "Forget about it. Dad says he wants to talk to you. He says you can call him collect at his place. All right?"

"Why don't you fuck with him a little, Mikey? Tell him Mom's already sold his car. That'll drive him crazy."

"Shut up about that, okay? Dad says you can call him collect."

"Maybe," she said. "Tell Mom I want some of that car, too."

"He really wants to talk to you."

"Maybe," she said. Then she said, "How's Ben Franklin anyway?"

"Ben's good."

"You're treating him right? He's getting enough water and food?"

"Yeah," I said. "I'm treating him right."

"Thanks," she said. "Later, Mikey."

Outside it was dark and the snow had become large and feathery and fell in thick sideways sheets. Ben was down at my feet, still munching away at the popcorn. I wondered when Mom would get home and thought about the car, a 1968 red Mustang, locked safely in Winnie Howell's garage on Breywick Street, three blocks away from our house. Mom and I had already talked about her plans to sell it and how she had a dozen or so offers. She was holding on to the car, waiting for the highest bidder now. It was a collector's item, worth I didn't know how many thousands. But I did know how much that car meant to Dad and I hadn't wanted her to sell it. She'd said, "How do you think we're going to pay for your mouth, Mikey? This Mustang's going to pay for your mouth—that's how."

I said, "I don't want it to pay for my mouth." We were driving the Mustang then, on our way to the orthodontist's for the first consultation, and I could smell the sweet treated leather of the interior, which, the year before, Dad had re-upholstered. Later, when he started asking about his car, Mom bought us a used Impala and hoarded the Mustang in Winnie's garage. Dad had redone the whole car at one time or another and usually spent his weekends working on it. He'd even named it—called it Victoria, after a famous queen of England, he said—and always spoke of it as a *she,*

she this and *she* that, until Mom would get irritated and tell him that a mustang wasn't a *she*. Sometimes he'd just call it "the horse" in this rough, affectionate man voice. The car was sort of alive to him. Mom was decked out in her best suit that day and I was in my good clothes, too, because she didn't want them thinking we couldn't afford the braces. As she talked on, her voice got pitched and angry.

"I can't pay for your mouth," she said. "I'm just a secretary. Your dad can't pay for your mouth—every dollar he touches turns to booze. Don't you want your mouth?" I put my hand to my face and felt the buckteeth, the crooked, hard ridge of little bones, the ugly, ugly mouth that I'd lived with for fifteen years, and I didn't know what to say. "You deserve straight teeth. Other kids have straight teeth, and I want my son to have straight teeth, too." Ever since she'd kicked Dad out of the house, Mom had become vocal about what we deserved. "Don't worry about him," she said. "He put more time, money, and care into this car than he ever did any of us." Then she slapped the steering wheel with both hands and said, "We deserve to look at least as good as this stupid car."

We had stopped at a light and she was looking at herself in the rearview mirror, touching up her hair and tracing the wrinkles along her mouth, when she said, "Oh Christ, I've become an old woman," a thing she'd been saying a lot lately. "At least you deserve to look good. It's too late for your old mom." She was crunching up her face and looking at the thick lines that formed.

"He might get better," I said.

"Get better?" She laughed. "Your dad's a sick man, Michael. He's been sick for years. He won't get better."

"He might," I said.

"He's a bottle man, Michael," she said. "He's not a family

man." She had learned phrases like *bottle man* at this group she attended on Wednesday evenings called Wives of Alcoholics. "We've got to start thinking about us, Michael. You and me." She was still crabbing up her face and looking into it. "I just wish I'd kicked him out before I got like this." She rolled down the window and tried to throw out a strand of gray hair she'd just pulled from her head. She was forty-three and hated us to look shabby. The hair kept blowing back into the car. Finally, she let it fall into her lap. "It's a question of money, you know. If we could afford it, we'd get me a face-lift, too." Then she paused and said, "Don't look at me like that, Mr. Judgmental." I guess my face told her pretty much what I felt. "We're not bad just because we want some nice things for ourselves, are we?" When I didn't answer, she pressed the point, "Are we?"

"No," I finally said. "I guess not."

She took my jaw in her hand and shook it gently. "We're going to get you fixed up, kiddo." By then, the light had turned green and the people behind us were honking.

The phone rang and, for maybe the fifth time that night, it was Dad. "Christ, Mikey. I just got off the phone with your sister. She told me what you and your mother are up to. She told me you were turning my car into braces."

I didn't say anything. I could hear my own breathing amplified and strange in the receiver. The line beeped and I said, "I've got to get that."

He said, "Don't you dare leave me on this—" But I did.

"Goddamn you, Sarah," I said.

She said, "Somebody's after me, Mikey." I could tell from her voice that she'd been crying.

I said, "What?" Then I said, "Why the fuck did you have to tell Dad?"

"Somebody's after me," she said again. "They want to hurt me 'cause I owe them money, right?"

"Don't cry wolf to me, Sarah." I didn't like the sound of her voice. It sounded small and frightened.

"I'm not shitting you, Mikey. It has to do with money, okay? I owe someone money and they're going to hurt me now."

I said, "Why did you tell Dad?"

Her voice got sort of happy then. "He's pretty pissed off, I bet."

"Yeah," I said.

"That bastard wouldn't let me call collect. He made me pay for the phone call."

Then she said, "You tell Mom that somebody's after me. You tell her that somebody wants to hurt me. Later, Mikey."

"It's a vintage car, Mikey."

"Sarah says somebody wants to hurt her."

"Do you know how much work I put into that car?" He was yelling.

I said, "I had ugly teeth."

"But the Mustang's my car. My car!" he shouted. I pulled the phone away from my ear and held it out in front of me; he sounded tiny and distant now. "My car! My car!" He became this little furious cartoon voice trapped in the phone. I could put him down on the table, if I wanted. So I did that. I put him down and walked away from him on my way to the bathroom. I heard his voice saying, "Mikey? Mikey? Where are you, Mikey?" He was pathetic. He was easy to hate now.

In the bathroom, I smiled in the mirror and saw that my gums were lined with a little bit of blood. The scarlet mound of a pimple was beginning to rise at the center of my forehead. I felt it beneath my skin: hidden and painful. Ben had followed me into the bathroom and climbed into the tub, where he liked to drink from the leaky faucet. I heard the small, wet sounds of him slurping away in there. "What are we going to do, Ben? What the hell are we going to do?"

I got back to the couch and turned the TV on, to this program about performing dolphins. I could still hear Dad's voice speaking through the receiver on the table. "Mikey . . . Mikey," it said. The program was called *Our Friends from the Sea* and a scientist with a mustache was saying, "I'm absolutely convinced that dolphins can understand us— every word we say. They have a marvelous talent for deciphering vocal structures." Then he turned away from the camera and looked at this dolphin in the pool beside him. The dolphin's head bobbed above the surface of the water. Its eyes were these sensitive black ovals, like polished stones. "You can understand me, can't you?" the scientist said, and the dolphin beeped and clicked at him.

The orthodontist's office was painted in shades of mint blue, clean and arctic, and smelled of toothpaste and harsh, soapy chemicals. In the waiting room, kids with headgear and silvery mouths sat beside their mothers. These kids didn't look happy, not exactly, though they did look changed. They looked stunned and maybe a little afraid. On the receptionist's counter—a cool slab of green—sat two plaster molds of corrected teeth, a plastic model of the human jaw, and a shiny bell to ring for the receptionist. One girl said to her mother, "Is he going to use that thing on me again?" The girl wore an apple green T-shirt with the word *Happening* in large yellow letters across her chest.

Her mother just said, "Your teeth are getting so pretty."

The orthodontist was called Dr. Ellis. His assistant was a Polish woman, Tasha, who spoke with a European accent and had this long bleach-blond hair and a nice straight smile and wore blue surgical clothes. It was our first visit, so Mom insisted on going back to the exam room with me. "We want to get on the two-year payment plan," she kept saying to Tasha. Mom was nervous. Her voice trembled a little. She didn't know what to do with her hands.

"You have to talk to the receptionist," Tasha said. She motioned for me to sit in one of those long chairs and pulled a tray of metal instruments up beside me. The instruments were bright and seemed unreasonably sharp and pointed; they clattered on the tray as Tasha moved it. Lulling violins played "Raindrops Keep Fallin' on My Head" from hidden speakers. I heard the scream of a girl coming from another room down the hall.

"Relax," Tasha said. She touched me on the shoulder. "We're not going to do anything that hurts today."

"Do they have braces in Poland?" I asked.

She laughed. "No. In Poland, the people are poor." Her eyes were the same shade of blue that covered the waiting room's walls. I imagined how Tasha had come to this country poor, with a brown potato sack over her shoulder, dust in her yellow hair, and a mud-puddle cast to her eyes. Then, simple as that, she'd cleaned herself up, gotten a job, and come into her bright, hard new-world beauty.

The chair buzzed and lifted me closer to the globular light that Tasha centered above me. She flipped the light on, snapped on a pair of latex gloves, and touched my mouth. The gloves smelled of mint and Clorox, and I started having these crazy thoughts about her. I saw Tasha and me in this dark blue minivan, with kids and the best downhill ski equipment in the back. With ungloved hands, she touched my face—my mouth was strong and symmetrical—as I drove up a bald, snowy mountain. The kids had bright alloy complexions like hers. "Michael," she said, "Michael."

I held her closely. I said, "We're going to have a great ski vacation this year. The kids are going to love it."

The doctor had entered the room, and Tasha seemed to disappear behind his tall shoulder. He introduced himself and said, "How you doing there, Mikey?" He had this large, fat man's laugh, even though he was slim and had a neat haircut and looked like a newscaster or a senator. (Later, in the car, Mom would say, "Dr. Ellis was handsome, didn't you think? Of course, he had to be wearing a ring. The handsome ones all do.")

"Call me Michael, please," I told him.

"He's got a difficult mouth, Mrs. Larsen," he told my mother. He moved my jaw from side to side, then up and down, and my bones made a light popping sound. "You've got a difficult mouth, Mikey," he said. "What a jaw . . . what a mandible," he said. Tasha seemed to agree. She was studying me with this focused, knowing eye.

"The kids teased him for years," my mom said.

"Please don't, Mom," I said.

I saw my mother looking over Tasha's shoulder. My mother was smiling and seemed extremely happy, as happy as she'd been since she kicked Dad out. "We've been wanting to do this for a long time now," she said. "We want to get on the two-year payment plan."

"He's a difficult one," Dr. Ellis said. My mouth felt small

and soft in his hands. His face moved so close to my own that I could smell through his cologne and spearmint breath to some salty, moist odor. "But nothing we can't fix."

"That's a relief," my mom said.

The doctor was working my jaw in this funny sideways direction, until I felt my bones lock.

"I'm afraid, Michael," he said, "that we're going to have to correct your jaw."

"What does that mean?" my mom asked.

"Well, Mrs. Larsen," he said, "it means that we're going to have to break it."

Dad was still on the phone. He was saying, "Please, Mikey . . . please. Just pick up the phone and talk to me." I picked up the phone, but I didn't talk to him. "Are you there, Mikey? I just want to talk to you, Mikey." His voice sounded tired. On the *Our Friends from the Sea* program, performing dolphins were being transported. These men wrapped the dolphins up in thick black slings and carried them into the backs of special air-conditioned trucks, then drove them onto the freeway. I couldn't help but imagine this terrible accident. I saw the truck burning and the slick, mercury-like bodies of dolphins flopping over the black asphalt as semis and cars tried to swerve around them.

"Dad," I said.

"Mikey," he said.

"Could you call me Michael instead of Mikey? I'm fifteen. I want to be called Michael now."

"Sure," he said. "I could do that. Look, Michael, I'm sorry about this. I didn't want you to get caught in the middle." He sounded sort of sad, and I liked the way it felt when he called me Michael, as if some weight, some realness, had been added to me.

"I know," I said.

"Look," he said, "maybe we could make a deal. Would you make a deal with me, Michael?"

"I don't know."

"Well," he said, "if you tell me where your mom parked my car, I'll pay for your braces."

I thought about this. "You don't have that kind of money, Dad." He was silent. I heard the grainy buzz of the line between us, and I wished I hadn't said anything about his money. Next to me on the couch, Ben huddled over his pink claws, absorbed in the minuscule task of preening them.

"Do you hear what you're telling me? This is me. This is your dad, your father, speaking. You're my son, Michael. You used to call me Daddy. We lived together in the same house for fifteen years." He wasn't shouting. I had heard him speak like this to Mom before. It was a kind of forceful begging. He sounded weak, dependent on me for whatever kindness I could show him.

I said, "Winnie Howell."

He said, "What?"

"The car's parked in Winnie Howell's garage."

"Thanks, Mikey. Thanks so much. We're going to take care of your mouth, all right?"

Then he hung up. I turned to Ben, who was staring into the TV screen—the glow of the colors could mesmerize him—and said, "I fucked up, Ben. I fucked up." The dolphins flew through hoops and performed back flips.

I rushed over to the refrigerator door and pulled down the numbers of Jim and Larry, the guys Mom was sort of seeing—not seriously, just dating. I called Jim's place and got an answering machine. At Larry's a little girl answered. I hadn't met Larry or Jim yet and didn't know this little girl. "Is my mom with your dad tonight?" I could have asked for Larry, but I didn't really want to talk to him.

She said, "I don't know. Who's your mom?"

"Marsha Larsen."

"I don't remember the name of the lady he's with. She's pretty, though."

I said, "She's got shoulder-length hair. It's black."

"That's not her," the little girl said. "This lady has short red hair."

I remembered that Mom had gone to the hairdresser that afternoon. She'd probably had a cut and gotten her color changed. "That's her," I said. "Is she there?"

The girl handed the phone over. "Hello."

"I told Dad about the Mustang."

"Who's this?" the woman asked.

"Michael," I said. "It's Michael." A key turned in the front door then and Mom walked in. She was with a man—probably Jim—and I said, "I'm sorry," to the woman on the phone and hung up.

The snow was really coming down now. It covered the streets and sidewalks, and the houses in our neighborhood were quiet, shut up inside the glow of their windows. On the walk from our place to Winnie's, Mom was edgy, excited. She kept slipping in her little pointy shoes and Jim had to hold her up. "Why did you have to spill the beans, Mikey?"

I said, "I don't want to talk about it in front of him."

She fell, and Jim picked her up. "Ouch! Ouch!" she said. Then she looked at me. "I don't think you're acting very grateful."

When we got to Winnie's, Mom said, "Ha! We beat him. We got here first." We were standing on the front porch in a halo of snowy light when Winnie answered the door. She was a skinny woman with curly dark hair and high cheekbones. "Bill's coming for the Mustang," Mom said.

Winnie Howell flipped on the yellow garage light, and the waxy red paint of the Mustang glowed as our nervous shapes glinted and slid across it. It was kind of miraculous how the car was still there, untouched, recoverable. "This *is* a beautiful car," Jim said. He was sort of caressing it. Jim had that newscaster look, like the orthodontist—aging, slim, and knowledgeable. He probably kept a decent bank account, too. Mom's new hairstyle was weird, cut close to her head, feathery and mulchy, so that her face seemed larger, crisp with makeup. She had been spending all sorts of money—for clothes, jewelry, hairstyles—on the strength of what the Mustang would bring in. Every time I glanced at her that night, I was shocked by how odd and different she looked, and I turned away again.

Mom slid into the driver's seat and started the car. Winnie said, "I don't want to be here when he arrives." She was shivering in the yellow light. At the mouth of the garage, the storm made a sucking sound.

"Get in," Mom said. "We'll all go out for a drink or something."

Mom craned into the windshield as she drove. "I can't see anything," she said. Normally, she wouldn't have driven in this weather, but she was determined to get the car out of the neighborhood, out of Dad's reach.

"Drop me off at home, please," I said. "I don't want to go for a drink."

"Party pooper." Mom's voice sounded mean. She slowed down and came to a stop in front of our home.

"Sarah's been calling," I said. "She says someone she owes money to is going to hurt her."

"She's just crying wolf," Mom said. Then her tone changed. She was trying to be nice, I guess. "Mikey got his braces on today. Show Jim and Winnie your braces, Mikey. Give us a smile." Jim and Winnie looked at me. Mom's face was a weird green color from the glow of the dash. I didn't want to show these strangers my teeth. But I did.

"Very handsome," Winnie Howell said in this fake voice.

On New Year's Day, three days after I'd had my jaw corrected, Dad showed up on the doorstep. Mom was at work. Sarah had already taken off, and I wore this huge bit in my mouth, with a space in it for a straw. My mouth would be wired shut for more than two weeks. I ate mostly thin milk shakes and soup and drank a lot of fruit juices, even though it hurt to suck on a straw. I couldn't talk. I carried around a pad and pen and I tried to communicate with these things. The world seemed extremely loud to me, full of noise and words, as if I had become some kind of silent focus where all this sound gathered and blared. It was strange to be home alone and hear the phone ring. Sometimes I answered it and heard the voice on the other end say, "Hello . . . hello. Is anybody there?" At these times, my mouth felt large and muzzled. "Helloooooo," the caller would say. I felt pushed away from them in this insulated world of silence and injury. Eventually they or I hung up.

I told myself that this would make a difference, that this would change something. I would have a straight, corrected mouth forever after this.

"Jesus, kid!" Dad said. "What happened to you?" I wrote the explanation out and showed the pad to him. He said, "Oh, braces. Good for you. Good for you." He was grief-stricken and wasn't worried about money or even about his car yet. He had lost his license for several months because of his poor driving record and wouldn't start wanting his car back until he knew that he couldn't have Mom. Then he wanted his car.

We took a cab to a diner called Lambs. Little woolly lambs stood on the front of the menus, cute and vulnerable-looking, despite the fact that they were also featured inside the menu as a dish. The waitress was very cautious—people pitied me, thought I was fragile—and set the milk shake in front of me as if it were an explosive. I waited for it to melt a little, thin down.

Dad said, "I'm trying to change. Tell your mother that, will you? I'm feeling under control. Look at me, Mikey. I look good, don't I?" He wore freshly laundered clothes and so much cologne that the abrasive scent of it hovered in the air—all things I was supposed to tell and tried to tell Mom later. But his face was swollen and his hands shook as he lifted his orange juice. "She's seeing other men, isn't she?"

I wrote "I'm sorry" on my pad and showed it to him.

"So she is seeing other men?"

I showed him the words on the pad again.

"Tell her that I'm going to that group—AA, right?— and that I sit there and say, 'My name's Bill and I'm an alcoholic.' Will you remember to tell her that?"

I wrote "Sure, Dad" and showed him the pad.

"Good kid," he said. He laughed. "How are you going to tell her anything? Look at you. You can't say two words." Then, right out of nowhere, he said, "I love you, kid," and I looked at my pad and pen and didn't know what to do with them.

When he reached out to touch my cheek, I blocked his hand with mine and wrote out another message: "Not my face, Dad. It hurts."

"Oh God, kid," he said, taking my shoulders and squeezing them so hard that I felt the trembling from his swollen hands enter me. "We'll be okay, won't we?"

I stood in front of my house, watching Mom and Winnie and Jim turn the corner in the Mustang, and thanked God I wouldn't have to sit around while they had their stupid drinks and asked me to smile for them.

When I walked in the front door, the phone was ringing. I knew it couldn't be Dad, not yet. He would be driving across the city in a cab. Ben had gone down to the basement, and, from the kitchen, I could hear him burrowing into some boxes. He was somewhere beneath me. I could hear the small, struggling sounds he made, creepy sounds, and I moved into the living room. Ben would disappear in the basement all night sometimes, not emerging until the next day. He liked the closeness of it, the dark down there.

It was Sarah on the phone. "Look," she said, "these people who want to hurt me have knives, Mikey. They may not kill me, but they're going to cut me."

I felt my face heat up. I hated her for doing this to me. "Don't give me that shit, Sarah. We all know what you're up to."

"Jesus, Mikey," she said. Her voice had become defensive and vulnerable. "What's your problem?"

I hung up the phone and started to put my hat and coat back on. I thought maybe Dad would be at Winnie's by now. I didn't want to talk to him and I didn't want him to see me, but I wanted to see him. The phone began ringing again. I closed the door and locked it. Outside, snow flurried in the bright circles of streetlamps. Trees bent sideways, cloaked in white. I put my gloved hands to my mouth because it hurt from too much goddamn talking.

At Winnie's, I stood behind some bushes across the street and waited. I felt the snow fall and gather on my lashes and hat and become heavy on my coat. The roads and walks and lawns lay buried and mute and the air was a chilly lunar color from all the white. The shapes of parked cars stood crystallized beneath snowdrifts. Everything had been softened, erased. Dad's cab pulled up and he stumbled out of it and ran to the garage door. A huge orange coat covered him up, its bright color burning in the white air. His footprints curved awkwardly through the snow. He was drunk, fucked up. He looked into the little windows of the garage, then looked away. "Oh God," he said. He pounded on the garage door.

I stayed behind the bushes. I thought of Tasha, Dr. Ellis's blond assistant, and how we could disappear together, live in abandoned school buildings and beneath docks in California, the way Sarah had disappeared with Marcus. Or maybe we would live in a house, the way people should live. A house on a stupid green hill somewhere. And I would learn her language, the only language we would speak together.

I had screamed a lot—I was conscious and could hear the bones in my face crack—when they broke my jaw. I screamed even though I felt nothing. I screamed at the distant snapping of my own bones. Dr. Ellis grimaced from the effort—my jaw hadn't broken easily. "We're going to make you a handsome set of teeth," he said. My face floated out into the room, rising to the ceiling because of all the dope they'd given me. Tasha stood behind Dr. Ellis, her blue eyes clear and glowing, beautiful, so beautiful that I knew I could never have her. I tried to picture it anyway—the green hill, the house in which we sat at our table in a roomful of yellow light, speaking to each other in her language. I spoke it perfectly, a stream of delicate foreign words coming from me as I said things to her, graceful and true things, that I could not imagine saying in any language that I understood.

CLEAN AWAY

It happened in a steak house somewhere near the Idaho-Nevada state line. I was with Ruby, my second girlfriend after my third divorce, on a long weekend trip to Bayview, Idaho, a little mountain town with a view of a lake, where we were going to try to save our relationship of five months. But we got caught in a blizzard and had to turn around.

That night we stayed in a little town with an Indian name I no longer remember. The motel was called the Apache. It had a TV, but the picture was bad. So we got ourselves a bottle of scotch and some ice and I told her I wanted it to work for us. I told her I was tired of February—of the cold, short days. I was tired of being lonely in Boise, where I managed a Tommy Tom's barbecue restaurant—a good, steady job, I reminded her. I opened the little box and showed her how the diamond sparkled in the yellow light of the motel room and said, "Please, Ruby, please." When that stone ignited in the palm of my hand, I felt young again, like I could afford new love. The dark outside stuck to the little window of our room, and we were reflected in its black glass. Ruby put on the ring without saying yes or no. Then we drank too much and I called her a bitch, later remembering only the anger and not the reason. We made love anyway, with the reading lamp throwing a dirty sheet of light over Ruby's face. The room stunk of Lysol and the liquor we had spilled on the carpet. I mounted her and looked away at the orange curtains. "It doesn't feel right if you do that," she said. "Look at me, please."

I looked at her. But Ruby kept her eyes open during sex, in a way that made me feel creepy and exposed. I asked her to close them, *please,* and she said, "I need to see you." So I looked away again, concentrating on a wide stain over the curtains while I came. Then I rolled over and lay on my back, breathing and feeling, for a moment that didn't last long enough, less like I needed to marry Ruby or anyone. It was an open, easy feeling inside me, as if a bird were flying in the wide spaces between my penis and my head and would never land.

In the morning the liquor pressed against my eyes. My body felt heavy and filled with dirty, tired organs. My penis was soft, but capable of ten thousand more stupid, desperate erections. I was forty-one and my mother was already dead. I remembered my two boys—my only kids—living in Salt Lake City with my second wife. But the thought of them did not make me feel proud or accomplished. The newest thing in my life then was a red Camaro I had just bought. It had dark tinted windows, a hood scoop, and a spoiler on the back. But now that the car was mine, I felt cold and unhappy toward it.

That morning, Ruby gave the ring back. She said, "I'm sorry, Gordon. But we weren't sober." She put her head in her hands and shook it. "My friends keep telling me to get out of this. They ask me if I enjoy being treated like shit."

We were standing out by the Camaro, and after Ruby said this, there was a long, awkward silence, out of which the dead yellow desert surrounding the little town seemed to roll into the February sky and on into Idaho. I felt the need to say something. "Love is complicated, Ruby." Ruby closed herself into the Camaro, and I sensed her, behind the dark glass, sitting in a space away from me. I didn't want to be in front of the Apache motel anymore. I got in and drove away from that place.

The way to Bayview was blocked by snow, so we decided to drive south to Reno. The silence between us was awkward. Once, I drove fast enough to scare her into speaking. "Please, Gordon. I don't like this. Slow down." I did—a little—but I didn't mind her being scared.

"I think we should talk," I told her. "That's why we came on this trip together."

She said, "I'm tired, Gordon. Just give me a little time." She dozed off and I watched her sleep. Her face was soft and beautiful until it began to twitch in a dream. Ahead, a dark blue storm built up. By the time Ruby woke, the storm had cleared and the land was mute and colorless with new snow. I imagined looking down on the red dot that was us breaking through the silent white plains of America. This gave me a large God feeling. But that was lonely. So I looked into the future and saw Reno—the felt tables and the whirl of slot machines. Blackjack dealers stood behind their chips, their eyes feline, like dark gems, and when they looked at you, your future felt small. But I remembered *chance*. I remembered that anything could happen in my country.

"Tell me something, Ruby," I said. "If I were a billionaire, would you marry me?"

She blinked at me slowly. Her eyes were still stupid with sleep. "I had scary dreams," she said. "Please don't be an asshole, Gordon."

So I gave her a few more seconds to recover. "I just want to hear the truth of it from you, hon. That's all."

She sighed and pulled up a fallen bra strap from inside her shirt. She was fed up with herself and didn't try to hide it. "I always fall for assholes. I don't know why, and there's nothing I can do about it, but I always end up with the assholes. And if an asshole had money, that might make him a little less of an asshole. You know what I mean, Gordon?"

What I loved about Ruby was the way she accepted things. She bent to the world and made me feel less anxious about trying hard. I hated to try hard. It wore me out and made me angry at everything. And I loved the way that she could dislike herself with such ease. Why wouldn't she have me? Why wouldn't she take me and give me children and a gentle future and something to work hard for?

"Like about how much do you think I would have to have to be less of an asshole?"

"Oh, Gordon, don't make me answer questions like that."

But I acted vulnerable and said, "Please, hon. I'd just like to have an idea of what your needs and wants are."

"A million," she said. "Maybe a little more or a little less. I don't know."

I put my sunglasses on and the world turned three shades grayer. I wanted to hide in the dark for a while.

We had been wrong about Reno: It was farther than we'd thought—still hundreds of miles down the interstate when we reached the steak house called Mom's, where the thing that I'm going to tell about happened to me. It was late afternoon and more bad weather had lumped up to the west and was moving in on us again. Inside the restaurant, candles in red glass jars shed a bloody light over the tables. Thick burgundy carpet covered the floors and walls. A huge velveteen depiction of a bullfight hung above the cold black pit of the fireplace. It was a dark, tender interior, like the inside of somebody's stomach. Except for a small family eating at one of the booths—a middle-aged man, an old woman, and a little girl—the restaurant was empty. As we passed the family, the girl looked up at me. Her eyes seemed dark, without any whites in them. We ordered steaks and scotch from a young blond waitress whose breasts were unpleasantly large, dangerously mounted on her small body, giving her a lopsided, unstable look. I felt bad for her and tried not to notice.

"Have as much scotch as you want, honey," I said. "After this, we're going to find us a Super-Eight and take the Jacuzzi suite just to make things special." I wanted her to look forward to a mildly drunk evening—just drunk enough to make us happy and to make our mood sexy. "We'll be good to each other tonight. I think we owe it to ourselves."

But Ruby was already on her second scotch, and it was starting to make her mean. "Don't think I don't see how you're looking at our waitress, you bastard."

"It's not what you're thinking," I told her. "It's just that—she's so—you know. . . ."

"It's just that you want to bang her, Gordon, isn't it?"

"Jesus, Ruby."

A few booths away from us on the other side of the aisle, the man was trying to feed the old woman. "Come on, Mother, you've got to eat your meat. You haven't taken two bites." He had cut her steak into tiny pieces and lifted the fork to her mouth. "Open up, Mother. Please, Mother."

"The problem with you is that you're not even human, Gordon. Look at me when I'm speaking to you. You're not capable of tenderness or care. You're not capable of basic, human things. You know that?" Ruby was drunk in a very unattractive way. The word *bitch* flashed through my mind again, but I told myself that I loved her and that everything would be all right if I could somehow convince her to marry me.

"You've got to eat. If you don't eat, I worry. All you do is make trouble for me. Now open up." The man seemed desperate, and I wanted that old woman to eat. I wanted the family to sit in peace. I thought that was very little to ask. I thought that the day could give me at least this one thing that I wanted.

"Where are you, Gordon?" Ruby held her head sideways in a hand above her drink. "You're sitting across from me, but you're somewhere else. You're not here, are you?"

I said, "I'm here. I'm here."

Our waitress came and placed our steaks in front of us and then stood back gazing at me. She wore this fearful, excited look. "You're Barry Manilow, aren't you?" I didn't say I wasn't. Ruby laughed in my face, but the waitress kept looking at me in a way that made me feel admired by a whole world of unknown people. I signed a menu for her. When she read my signature, she said, "You spelled your own name wrong," and she walked away, knowing that I was a liar.

"You poor thing, Gordon. You're so desperate." Ruby laughed and cocked her finger at me, which was her way of saying she had you. "It's those sunglasses. They make you look less worthless, Gordon. You could almost be a famous person."

"Look, Ruby, I don't need to hear this kind of talk from you right now. I'm trying to feel good about myself, and you've got me all wrong. I care for you, hon. Give me a little credit, all right? Now let's not think about the past.

Let's think about right now. Let's be decent to ourselves and have a good time." I put out my hand. I wanted us to shake on it.

"Jesus, Gordon. You sound so sappy."

I stood up. "I have to take a piss, all right?"

The bathroom was small, lighted by a naked bulb. I stood above the toilet in the smell of urine and ammonium chloride, holding myself and slowly realizing that nothing was going to come. It was going to be an unsuccessful piss. Across from me, in a cracked mirror, I saw that Ruby was right about the sunglasses. There was something suddenly gorgeous about my jaw, something valuable and glistening about the lower part of my face now that the upper part was canceled by two chilly lenses of mirrored glass. I got that God feeling again—powerful and distant—and kept it as I walked back into the restaurant and sat down across from Ruby. "I'll be whoever the hell I want to be," I said. "I'll be Barry Manilow. I'll be anybody I want."

Her face had a happy, conniving expression, as if she knew a hell of a lot more than I ever would. "Our neighbors heard the little exchange with the waitress, Gordon. Only they didn't hear the last part." She laughed. "They just heard that you were famous and they want you to sign their napkins or something."

I looked over at them and saw the man motioning and waving for me to come join them.

"What you waiting for, Gordon?"

"All right," I said. "You want to come with maybe?" I hated to meet new people alone.

"It's all yours, star," she said, cocking her finger at me again.

I chased a bite of steak down with some scotch, then got up and left Ruby.

"Hi," I said.

We shook hands, and before I could say anything, he lowered me down next to him in the booth. He was a little overweight, balding—his naked pate shone like polished copper in the red light—and he smelled of the steak he was still chewing as he spoke to me. "So, we heard that you were Barry Manilow."

I didn't say anything.

"We really appreciate you coming over here to talk to us."

The girl sat across from me, holding a naked Barbie doll in her arms. She might have been five. She said she had met a famous person in a restaurant before—Ronald McDonald. He had given her a coloring book. Did I have anything to give her?

I put on a fake smile. "I'm sorry," I said. When her face went sad, I pulled out a dollar bill and gave it to her.

"Hey," the man said. "You don't have to give us money." So I took it back, and the little girl cried.

"Jesus," I said. "This isn't working. Look, I'm not really anyone, okay?" I took my sunglasses off and showed him. "I'm sorry, pal."

"Oh," he said. His face lost its color and his smile left. He put his head in his hand, like it was just more dead-weight to hold up, and said, "Well, who are you, then?"

"Gordon," I said.

"Gordon?" he said, as if the bite of steak he'd just put in his mouth didn't taste right. And I had to agree with him. That name didn't sound like there was much of anything on the other side of it.

"Yeah," I said, "Gordon."

"Look, it's not as if I'm anyone, either. Shit, my name's

Dave. Dave," he said again, putting out his hand. We shook, meeting each other a second time. "So what is it that you do, Gordon?"

I looked for a way out of the conversation that was about to happen. But Ruby had grabbed the waitress and was telling her a few troubling things over at our table. "Did you see the way my boyfriend was looking at you?" she was saying. "He's about as slithery as they come."

"Restaurant management," I said.

"Got woman troubles, uh?"

Ruby was talking pretty loudly, and Dave and I could hear everything she was saying.

"I'd rather talk about restaurants, if you don't mind."

"Restaurants," he said. "Well, I'm a steak lover myself. But I'm sort of sick. The old ticker don't tock so well."

"Talk?" I said.

He patted his fat chest and began taking out lots of little pills from lots of little pill bottles. "My heart, you know."

"Sure," I said.

"The doctor says that Daddy shouldn't eat steak. But he eats steak anyway."

The girl seemed to like me enough now to talk to me again.

"You bet," he said, "I love steak. And I'd like to know how they can ask a sick man to keep on living without the things he loves."

He was selling a kind of superpowered cleanser now and eventually wanted to break into Amway products—selling tube socks and things out of his home. From a bag next to him, he took out a bottle of the stuff he sold. CLEANAWAY, it said in large, scary red lettering.

"All this cleaning power for only nineteen ninety-nine.

You make a stain, Gordon, any goddamn stain you want—
chocolate, berries, blood, wine, vomit—any goddamn stain,
and this'll clean it right up."

But he sounded angry when he said that, and I wondered
why his own white shirt was marked by what seemed to
be old, soiled-in food stains.

"She," he said now, looking at his mother, "won't eat two
bites of her steak. Good Idaho beef, and she won't take two
bites." The old woman didn't say anything. She sat next to
the girl in a sort of trance, looking down at the unfinished
meat on her plate, so that I could see only her bun of flaxen
white hair. "Well, I will," he said, taking her plate and
huddling over it, sopping the bloody juices up with a hunk
of bread and forking the nuggets of cut steak into his
mouth.

I looked over at Ruby again, hoping to get away from
Dave finally, but she was still speaking to the waitress. "He
made me feel like a mud puddle last night," she was saying.
"A woman wants to feel like a lake. She wants to feel like
an ocean. Am I right? But instead, I feel like a dirty creek
with his little minnow waddling up me."

I tried not to hear her and reminded myself that I was
meeting somebody and I liked him—sort of—and he
seemed to like me and I was feeling like, Who the hell
really needs Ruby?

"Woman trouble," Dave said, exposing a mouthful of
dark meat and bread. "You got it. And let me tell you,
Gordon, I know what that's like. Six months ago my wife
went batty and left me. She just stopped buying groceries
and let the milk rot in the fridge and our little Lilly here
run wild and the toilet bowl turn brown. Brown!" he said
again. "She called me a little boy. Do I look little to you,
Gordon?" I shook my head. "Well, she thought so. She said

she wasn't the whole world's mother. The last thing she needed, she said, was a fifty-year-old boy." He was getting excited as he spoke, a little short of breath and wheezy, and his face grimaced.

"You okay?"

"I'm not little, am I?" he asked.

In fact, the word for what Dave was was *fat*. He was fat, unhealthy, lonely, and living somewhere—he hadn't said where yet—in Idaho, which was the gray, snowy emptiness outside our window.

"No," I said. "You're not little, Dave."

He popped a few more pills and opened a packet of Alka-Seltzer into his water. "I kind of wish I hadn't eaten that second steak." He stacked the plates, pushed them away from him, and gave me a look of honest regret.

"Who's there?" The old woman looked up and began staring at me. Her skin jiggled and a web of saliva shimmered inside the oval of her mouth. "Who's there, David?" She must have been mostly blind. "Is that your brother Luke? That's you, isn't it, Luke?" Her hand paddled toward me, opening and closing and roaming in the air until it found my cheek. It smelled soapy and clean and was surprisingly warm. "My baby," she said.

"Oh Christ," Dave said. He removed her hand and reminded her, almost yelling now, that his bother Luke had been dead for years. This made his mother moody, and she sat up in her chair and asked to speak to a woman named Jamie.

"Damn it, Mother," Dave said now, his face going scarlet. "Jamie's gone. Six months ago, remember? Gone." He spelled it out to her. "G-o-n-e."

"Jesus," I said to him. His coppery pate had just gone an unnatural color of white. "You don't look good, Dave."

"I'm okay," he said.

"You're not okay, man."

"I'm okay. I'm okay." He was holding on to his water glass and the chalky water at the bottom of it was shaking.

I got up and walked over to where Ruby was sitting. The waitress had finally gone, and Ruby was playing in her dinner salad, building soggy green piles on her plate. "I think we've got an emergency over here. I think someone is having an attack."

"What?" she said. She slowly got to her feet and stood there wobbling.

"Hey, miss." I flagged the waitress down and we met back at Dave's table.

"Look at him," I said. "He's not well."

But his face had recovered some of its normal color. "I'm fine," he said. "I just need to take a little bathroom break is all." He stood up to go, then collapsed over the table, his face landing in his daughter's dinner plate. French fries flew into the air and he made a sound like air going out of something for the last time. The waitress screamed and ran into the kitchen. The little girl had pulled her knees up beneath her chin and was crying. The old woman craned her head in no particular direction and felt the air with her hands. "My boy," she said. "What's happening to my boy?"

His body slid from the table to the floor of the restaurant, where he lay on his back now, the white balls of his eyes showing in a way that said he was dead. The waitress came out of the kitchen with the cook, her large breasts shifting with panic. A lighted cigarette stuck out of the cook's mouth and his long blond hair was gathered in a net. He was just a kid—maybe eighteen. "Shit," he said. "Do something, man. Pound on his chest or something."

"Yeah, Gordon," Ruby said. "You can't just do nothing."

"I don't know how," I said. But I did, kind of. I had taken a first-aid course six months ago, which the bosses at Tommy Tom's required of their managers and which I had not done so well in. I knelt down, pried his mouth open with my hands, plugged his nose up, and breathed into him the way I sort of knew it was done. Then I moved down and pumped on his chest with my fists. His weight felt solid and reinforced, like the weight, I guess, of a dead thing.

"Goddamn," the cook said. "He knows what he's doing. You know what you're doing, man." I kept working on him, pumping and breathing for him and thinking, for that moment, that maybe I could do this for another person, maybe I could save a life.

"He's dead, Gordon. Leave him alone now," Ruby said.

"The hell he is," I said. When I felt his tongue shoot into my mouth, I sat up.

"He's fucking breathing," the cook said, lighting himself another cigarette. "You saved his life."

Dave started coughing up his meal and I rolled him on his side and looked out the window at the blurry racks of red and blue lights whirling from the hoods of emergency vehicles.

"All right, guy, up we go." Someone lifted me to my feet. It was the ambulance people. They had descended on him and began performing complicated, painful-looking procedures. Somebody took me by the arm and walked me into a dark corner of the restaurant, away from everything.

I returned. "Hey!" I said. "You can't do this to me. I kept him from dying."

Ruby grabbed me and we faced each other. But I no longer knew what was appropriate between us, what to say and how to talk to her. "What you did was exciting." She was still drunk. "Let's find a place where we can go, Gordon."

I said, "Ruby, something important happened here." I put the keys to my Camaro in her hand. "I'm going with him. Maybe you should go ahead and take yourself back to Boise."

The family had deserted their table. I searched the restaurant until I found a group of emergency people and then walked into their tight circle. "My family," I said. "Where are they?"

"Sir . . . sir?" A woman in uniform restrained me. They had hooked him up to little bottles of liquid and were rolling him on a gurney into the purple evening now.

"Please. I'm his brother," I said.

"Then you ride in the car with your family." She pointed to where the mother and daughter sat in the back of a police car.

"No," I said. "You don't understand. He could die." I walked past her, somehow found the open doors of the ambulance, and climbed in. The light in there was a brilliant orange, as if I'd come to the hot core of something. I saw Dave's stocking feet—they had taken his shoes off—sticking over the gurney's edge and heard a machine helping him breathe.

"Hey, you can't do that. I'm sorry." Two paramedics crouched over Dave. The skinnier one, who had just talked to me, was about to poke a needle—so large, you didn't want to see it—into Dave's fat arm.

"Just let him sit," his partner said. "I'm not sure our guy is going to make it." He held Dave's wrist in his hand, taking his pulse.

"We can't let you ride with us, sir."

"Just let him sit, all right?" his partner said again. He took me by the arm and buckled me into a little seat in the back. "Sit tight, buddy."

The siren screamed. I cracked the curtain and saw the interstate falling away behind us and the last minutes of day burning out. We passed a station wagon full of children pointing at us as the mix of blue and red flashing lights fell on them and discolored their faces. I felt good. I sat at the tightening knot of disaster, of frantic speed and light and screaming. There was not much time now. This was an emergency. Something valuable was dying. Life mattered. Outside the light was finally dead. My face stared back at itself in the black window. It looked shocked and pale, ghostlike in the glass, and it scared me a little. I thought it might start talking to me, telling me things I didn't want to hear. I could see only the constricted holes of car head-lights on the other side of the window, gouging at the dark and burning through the picture of my sick face, and I didn't feel so well anymore.

A man with a bloody towel pressed to his forehead had just been rushed into a swinging door when I arrived at the hospital. I stood in front of the old woman and the little girl in a white hallway. A fat woman dressed in a pink sweatsuit and taking up two plastic waiting room chairs was the only other person there. I couldn't see what her emergency was and wondered if there was something wrong inside of her, at the center of her huge pink body. I hoped for it, because we began to seem like the only emergency in Idaho. I wanted there to be more injured people, a small mob of desperation and bright hysteria, anything to keep this strange blur of urgency going. A woman doctor sprinted by in sneakers, the wings of her lab coat flapping as she turned the corner and disappeared in white light. I looked for some softer color and found the little girl's yellow dress. But when I walked up to her, she turned away to talk to her doll in a space that was safe from me.

"Luke . . . Luke?" The old woman's head pivoted. She was lost and I wanted to help her find herself. I wanted her to know I was there.

"Here I am."

Her face saw me, then pulled away. "I don't know you," she said.

I headed toward the glass doors of the exit at the other end of the hall. But it seemed like a very long walk. On the way, a doctor stopped me. He was dressed in the green fatigues of a surgeon and was wiping his hands and forehead with a cloth so white, it seemed to burn with a fluorescent, chemical heat.

"I'm very sorry, Mr."—and he called me by a surname that I decided to forget forever. "I'm very sorry."

Outside the night was close around me and pressed down on the road where I walked. Toward morning, the sky turned a deep blue—like a huge feeling that I could not see the end of—until I began to think that I was at the bottom of it, making the universe pulse and ache. I thought about praying and almost called out the name of God—but what name would that be?—when Ruby pulled over and I saw, in the purple morning air, the red Camaro, which really was, when you thought about it, as good as anything else to call your own. Ruby leaned over, opened the door for me, and I climbed out of the cold morning and into her arms. Yes, I told her. He would be just fine. They were transferring him to his hometown hospital and he would live on for some years more. The sun rose like a piece of smashed fruit as Ruby began the six-hour drive to Reno. "You're all right, Gordon," she said. And later that day, my fourth marriage happened, a little longer and a little better than the other ones.

Rose

On her seventy-seventh birthday, Rose's husband for fifty-nine years, Maj. Riggs Glover, who hadn't done much for the last two decades but take long walks when the weather was good and carve pieces of wood into angels and statues of his favorite presidents—George Washington and Ronald Reagan—surprised her terribly by beginning, much more gently and suddenly than she had ever expected, to die across from her at a table in her favorite restaurant. Her immediate response was, "How dare you, Riggs Glover! Not on my birthday!" It was just like him to crush her heart in a season of joy, when she felt like coddling and nesting on the little things in life that brought her pleasure. He could be so tragic, casting shadows in her sunshine, as when, almost fifty years ago, she received on Easter Sunday a hand-delivered telegram from a colored soldier, anxious and embarrassed by the bad news he bore, informing her that her husband, Lt. L. R. Riggs Glover, air force pilot, had been downed in a region of the world whose name was terrible, foreign, and Communist-sounding to her, impossible even to pronounce as she felt her heart turn to the soft, muddy place where her husband's grave would dig itself even on Easter, when everybody in Springfield, Tennessee, nodded at one another in the blue morning wash of sun to say, "Hallelujah, Christ has risen!" For weeks, women friends brought her the sad cakes they had baked and drove her to church, where the congregation began to treat her, as a new widow, with an unpleasant and distant respect because her quiet pain scared so many women whose husbands were also in Korea. And sometimes, to her shame, she did wish it: She wished all their husbands dead if only she could have Riggs back. Seven weeks later, they found him naked in the Communist wilderness, eating roots, insects, worms, and the meat of whatever he could kill. So they brought him back to Springfield, skinny and nearly mute with fear, where he spent the rest of his nights in Rose's bed, sometimes screaming out of his dark dreams because of all the soul scars that killing other men had given him, and she cared for him, woke him, and turned on the bedside lamp—because the dark scared him now—and whispered love into his blank face, even though she had not always been the kind of woman who could comfort the weakness in men. Instead, as an attractive young woman, she had been demanding of her admirers, feeling in herself only a limited amount of mother love—that indiscriminate, swollen affection for frail things. She had met Riggs at eighteen, attracted by his uniform, his boastfulness, and the way he seemed to dedicate all his masculine power to the respect of women . . . to her as a woman. He was a pilot, and she imagined him in his element—the purity of air—while she, Rose Waters, knew only the long brown busted-open fields of Tennessee—the dirty earth where her life had happened. He called her "my flower," and his idea of sex was clean, literary, flattering to her. "I could only ever love a woman whose name was a flower name, whose name was yours, Rose," he told her. Not that she didn't make him struggle.

Poor Riggs struggled, pleaded six months for the final gift
of her virginity, a gift that Pleasant Grove Baptist Church
had taught her to give only in matrimony, forcing him to
say, "With us, Rose, it will be holy, I promise. How could
such a love ever soil us?" Of course she'd been a virgin
then, at least sort of, there being only one other small incident, which she chose to forget now that she was seventy-
seven and Riggs had left her. For an old woman has rights
against her own history, Rose thought. So yes, she'd been a
virgin until one afternoon the way he sectioned an orange
at Plower's Field—something about his delicious fingers
gently dividing the fruit from its tight, greedy bundle of
light and sugar to feed slice after slice to her open mouth—
tempted her and they rolled away from their picnic, Riggs
wriggling and slipping off her, stupid as a dying fish, wearing, even in the blush of their first sex together, his air force
beret, his hat, because Riggs could do nothing in the world,
even this, without a hat on his head. Then she knew, by
the way he quickly spilled the mess of his pleasure outside
her, that he was the true virgin. Poor Riggs. Afterward, he
apologized, though he could barely speak, and she saw for
the first time something small and perishable in his eyes—
something frightened of the world's harsh light—that
taught her that she, a woman, had at least enough mother
love for her sad pretender, a large man, an air force pilot,
with something tiny and terrified inside him, whom Rose
Waters married at eighteen. Then, as soon as the children
came, they died. The first one turned to sadness and spilled
out of her, though it felt to Rose as if it were her heart that
had burst out from between her legs and exited forever.
The next two lived just long enough to be named, their
small lives exploding quietly in the night, silencing the
names that Rose would, in her latest years, choose to forget

because an old woman alone in the world should be allowed
to spare herself a certain amount of pain. Next, the war
came and went, and perhaps it was better never to have
been successful with children now that she had the night-
mares of her husband to care for. But those, too, passed,
because time smothers things slowly—everything—and
they bought a store in the Springfield town square and
called it Glovers, and though they would never be rich, they
would always have enough, which Rose's women friends
with children told her to be grateful for. And Rose was
grateful. During all this, time did not exactly pass, but stood
still and expanded, allowing more and more small, unim-
portant things to happen and fill the widening spaces of
Rose's life. Riggs took long walks by himself and began to
carve—at first ducks and geese and other North American
fowl, then his favorite American presidents, and finally, as
he worked less and less at the store and politics no longer
mattered to him, angels of all sorts—fat Italian cherubs as
well as powerful-looking adult angels, angels of revelation
and retribution. He set his chestnut and oak figures everywhere around their little house, as if for protection. So carv-
ing became his art and Riggs became an artist, and Rose
never pried into this quietest part of her husband, never
asked, Why angels, Riggs? Are you afraid of something?
though she knew that he and she and everyone was. She
volunteered at the school board and spent time with her
friends in the afternoons and even taught English, evenings,
at the Latino Cultural Center in Nashville, driving the forty
miles into the city in their boatlike Pontiac. She always felt
like there were things to do—little adventures of charity
and grace. She helped friends die and read for blind people
and told how the spring bloomed outside to people too
sick and immobilized to see for themselves. And as time ex-

panded, Riggs's and her love grew small and constant. The
endearments they called each other became names of favorite foods. She called him "sweetcakes" and "dumplings" and
he called her "my apple," which she much preferred to "my
flower," because what man called his wife "my apple" save
for her Riggs? So time had made him more original in his
love. And then finally, all of Rose's history, all of her life in
Springfield, as well as in the other small towns where
Riggs's short air force career had taken them, seemed to
arrive at the beginning of her seventy-eighth year, when
Riggs surprised her and gave her her last great pain by
dying on her birthday, for which Fae Marney, her best
friend for fifty-five years, came all the way from Knoxville,
and Rose's two living brothers, Burton and William Waters,
came from Georgia, and even some of Riggs's kin—his sisters, Margaret and Ethel, and their husbands—drove long
distances just to celebrate and share in her joy, God bless
them. Altogether, they made a motorcade of four large cars
driving to Mow's, her and Riggs's favorite catfish and fried-
chicken restaurant. And there, in the orange evening sun of
late spring that shone through the windows and made
Riggs's wrinkled face appear molten and oddly soft, he insisted on wearing his fishing cap crowned with the dark
barbs of hooks and complained of feeling unwell before he
could even take a bite of his favorite slaw, made with vin-
aigrette instead of mayonnaise dressing, just the way he
liked it, when his right hand—the one holding the fork—
fell into the large helping of mashed potatoes and gravy on
his plate and he said, "Oh God, Rose. My hand . . . my
hand." Not only the hand he ate with but also the hand her
poor pretender, her poor Riggs, carved his angels with. He
teetered then and seemed, in his last moments, afraid,
clumsy, and virginal again, as on the day he'd made a mess

of their first love together, before the stroke rose up and destroyed the little bit of water that was the rest of his soul on earth and knocked him to the floor of Mow's, leaving Rose, at the beginning of her newest and oldest year, to be nobody's apple. Oh Riggs . . . dear Riggs.

ICELAND

Sarah arrived in Florence late on a summer afternoon. The air smelled of fuel and spoiled food and it was so hot that the stone walls dripped and the yellow light shimmered like foil. In the streets, children ran half-naked and jumped into a large fountain, above which a Greek-looking statue of a man stood holding a trident. She walked sideways because of the weight of her bag and felt weak and tired and nearly incapable of hunting for a cheap hotel room. A man approached her—he seemed to walk out of nowhere—an Italian who spoke perfect English with a British accent. The accent impressed her—she was from North Dakota. It made her think of cooler climates, of decency and good manners and those unarmed, benevolent policemen who wore cone-shaped hats and blew shrill whistles in the streets of London.

"May I?" he asked.

"No," Sarah said. "That's all right."

"Please," he said. He put his hand out. He smelled of laundered cottons, of tonics and rosemary and orange liqueur. His face was long and narrow and his eyes were dark, like polished stones.

She had fantasized about doing something irresponsible

like this and now she did it. She handed him her bag with
the two brass zippers that jingled like change when she
walked. It was the middle of the day; if he turned out to
be cruel, she would scream.

They began walking down the crowded streets and the
crowds seemed to part for them. When he asked her about
herself, she immediately began lying. Her lies were extrav-
agant and alarmed her a little.

"My father was in the diplomatic corps," she said. "We
lived in many places." She listed a lot of these places, careful
not to mention White Plate, North Dakota. She did not
mix any truth with her lies. Her lies were pure and dark.
"But our favorite place was Iceland. We loved that country
more than any other."

"Iceland?" he said. He must have been in his mid-thirties.
Still, she noticed a sudden boyishness in his face. He was
curious. He wanted to know more about her. "Do you speak
the language?"

"Icelandic?" she said. "Oh, yes. We lived there for years.
My first boyfriend was Icelandic. I read Shakespeare in that
language." She laughed uncomfortably. He must have
known these were lies. But he didn't let on. Maybe his manners were too good for that.

"Speak some Icelandic for us," he said. They walked
through narrow stone streets that smelled of urine and
lemon peels. Everywhere in the city, the stone buildings
were the shabby brown color of history.

Icelandic was an easy language to invent. It felt like but-
terflies coming off her tongue. "I said," she said, "that Italy
is a generous country."

He took her to a beautiful hotel where the man behind
the front desk seemed to love him in that loud Italian way.
They gestured as if they were directing traffic and their

feminine manner—emotive and silly—put her at ease. The hotel clerk was balding and pudgy and his gray mustache was as fat as a bird. He said "pretty girl" to her in a heavy Italian accent that made him seem harmless and a little stupid.

Their room number was 317. Before she entered the room with him, she decided to let this happen. The sun was muted by drawn curtains that emitted a lavender-colored light. The bed stood in the center. It was high and canopied and white and its headboard was huge and embellished with fine touches of architecture and its thick oak frame smelled like a forest.

She tried to say his name in proper Italian but could not. The consonants were soft and the vowels were fast water in her mouth. She tried and tried to say it until the pretense that she had any linguistic talent whatever was up. He must have seen her lies now. Nonetheless, she lied to him about her name, too. One last beautiful lie, she thought. She called herself Margaret, a French name that came out of her mouth like a long sheet of fabric. He said it back to her in his strange accent and she felt rare and different from herself. She felt purely imagined, as if she had entered a story.

He took her from behind, which she had not expected from someone whose manners were so refined. He gently pushed her into one of the hulking bedposts, entering her more deeply and saying her name into her ear—Margaret—and caressing her breasts and the back of her thighs. He kept saying her name as if this were another way of entering her, and she tried not to remember White Plate, North Dakota. She tried not to remember her mother laundering her father's and little brother's clothes—folding their briefs from the Valley City JCPenney into stacks as white as chemicals. She tried not to think of Eddy, her ex-boyfriend, and

Eddy's father's truck, which stank of cigarettes, hide, and muddy boots. A bumper sticker on the tailgate said, NUKE 'EM. Another said, I WAS MADE IN AMERICA. YOUR IMPORT CAN'T SAY THAT. This was supposedly the voice of the Chevy truck speaking, which was weird, very weird. A year ago, as a senior at White Gate High, she had lost her virginity in that truck. She had gone down on Eddy in that truck, her knees and calves scraping against the pop-tops, gum wrappers, and the torn pages of *Sports Illustrated* littered over the mats. At first he tasted unexpectedly of corn chips, until he arrived at his moment. Then he tasted, Sarah supposed, like all men must taste, a bland, universal taste that finally taught her nothing. Weeks afterward, when she saw Eddy's father driving through the streets of White Plate, poised before the wheel, his face an older, rougher version of Eddy's, she wanted it back. Her name and number were in the boys' stalls in White Gate High. The message said, SARAH GREENLY TRUCKS. It's what her mother might have called "the story." That's how that story goes, her mother might have said. I could have told you that one myself. That's the oldest story in the book. Her mother had wide hips, short curly hair like wood shavings, and blue eyes that had sunk years ago into the rough grain of her skin.

Her orgasm began in a slow fault line down the middle of her body. She felt sweeping and vast, like one of the landscape paintings she had recently seen in European museums, with blue sky disappearing at the far corner of the world and with tiny farmers—so minute, it was almost impossible to think of them—working the huge green land. Nonetheless, Sarah thought of them. She imagined the small houses where they lived, the meals they took together, their soup as black as mud and smoking, the invisible patterns on the women's dresses, the cat the color of old wood curled in the recess of a window, the smells of clay and shit in the air, the spiderwebs in the barn and the buckets of well water, and the thoughts of the farmers and the women and children, the secret thoughts that made their lives worth something. The alternative—not to imagine them at all— seemed cruel. She would not want that to happen to her life.

Afterward, sitting on the balcony, her Italian lover produced a pearl-handled knife. For an instant, she was terrified. She expected to be punished now. But he halved an orange with it and they each ate the pulp out of their halves before he put the knife away. The distance was jigsawed with rooftops and spires, and, on the far edges, the barrels and stacks of industry glimmered and infected the sky with pink. Below, in the courtyard, old men sat in the shadows of oddly shaped trees, eating tiny purple grapes from bowls and playing a game with colored checkers. They considered each move and, from time to time, fingered their gray facial hair in a slow, loving way. Some chewed on cigars, while the air around them curled with smoke. They drank out of little metal cups and looked into the blue air and then considered the contest in front of them again.

"Should I tell you about our history?" he asked her.

"I already know about it," she said.

"It is a very violent and entertaining history," he said.

"I know that," she said.

"Many different families poisoning one another at supper. The dinner table was a frightening place in our Italian past."

"No," she said. "I don't want to hear about that."

Then she said, "I guess you do this with other girls." She crossed her legs, still feeling the pleasant sensation of having been entered, still feeling a residue of touch on her breasts and thighs.

"Do you really want to talk about that?" He smiled slowly. "Tell us more about Iceland."

He was more generous than she had expected. He was going to allow her to be as flagrant and fictitious as she wanted. "The first thing you need to know is that the name is a lie," she said. "Iceland is green as far as you can see. It is green all year long and so flat and treeless that you can see from one town to the next and, in certain places along the continent, from one coast to the next. And even though trees don't grow, wildflowers do. They are always at your feet. . . ." She kept talking now, hoping that she would not run out of lies before evening, hoping she could lie the time away until dinner, until sundown, lie until she would wake much later that night and leave him, still asleep in the huge white bed, to catch a night train.

"Tell us," he said, "what it is like to be the daughter of a diplomat."

"Oh," she said, "lonely. It's really very lonely." He stopped smiling then, his face registering the same blank shock that she felt at having run so quickly into even the smallest truth.

THE TROUBLED DOG

Benny knew that his mother was driving too fast. They had just begun the long trip from California to Montana, where they would visit his grandparents for Thanksgiving, and Jeannie was weaving their blue Impala in and out of traffic, accelerating until the air beat against the car. Benny fastened his seat belt and looked at the faces of the other drivers. They seemed shrunken behind their windshields, shocked and worried as the Impala sped past. "Momma," he said, "I think we're speeding."

She was trying to light a cigarette now, but couldn't because her hands were shaking. "We got to get to Grandma's by tomorrow. You don't want to spend Thanksgiving in this car, do you?"

Bo shouted from the backseat. "You're a bad driver, Momma."

Benny turned around to face his little brother. Bo was short for a boy of seven and had a hard time holding himself up in the seat because his feet didn't quite reach the floor. He sat crouched over Black, their family dog, feeding the animal Cheez Whiz and crackers. "Shut up, Bo," Benny said. "Momma drives fine. And stop feeding Black. I already told you not to feed the dog *people food.*"

"Shut up yourself," Bo said. "Momma is too a terrible driver. The dog in the dog movie is a better driver than you," he shouted over the seat into his mother's ear. He began to talk about his favorite movie, *The Shaggy Dog,* which he owned on video and had watched countless times before their old VCR at home broke down. In the movie, a high school boy tells his mother one day that he wants to be a dog, without school, homework, and house chores, then wakes the next morning to find his wish fulfilled. "Don't you think the dog in the dog movie drives a lot better than Momma can, Benny?"

"Quiet, Bo. Momma drives fine. She drives better than the dog. So don't start with that." Benny didn't want to talk about dogs with his little brother again. His little brother had wrong, horrible ideas about dogs.

"Let's not talk about the dog movie, hon. Quiet time now," their mother said. Her face was in a thick twist of smoke from the cigarette she had just managed to light. "Please, Bo. No dog talk. Not today."

As usual, Bo wasn't listening to anything that Benny and his mother said. "It's the best movie in the world, Benny. The way the dog can talk and the way the words come out of its mouth and the way it drives the car—that's my favorite part."

"Dogs don't drive and dogs don't talk. It's a stupid movie," Benny said.

"How do you know they can't talk? Maybe some dogs can."

"Dogs can't talk, Bo."

"Can so. Black can talk. Black tells me he's our—"

"Don't say it, Bo!" their mother shouted from the front seat.

Benny heard the raw anger in her voice and wished that

his stupid little brother would shut up. Bo told Benny and his mother things that neither of them wanted to hear. He told them how Black talked to him and what Black said. Black said things that you would think a dog might say to a little boy. He said, *I need to pee.* He said, *Feed me, love me, hold me.* He said, *I'm scared.* But he told Bo other things that no dog would say. Sometimes he said, *I'm your father, Bo.*

"Dogs do too talk," Bo said now. "Right now, Black's talking to me. He's saying he's hungry and he wants to stop and eat. Right now, he says. He's hungry. He wants to eat, you hear?"

At the restaurant where they stopped for lunch, Benny stared out the window to where Black was tied up to the car door, howling and fighting against his leash. His mother was counting the cash she had—about fifty dollars—and Benny was trying to calculate how much they would need for gas and food on their trip. He was only eleven and wasn't sure about the cost of things, though he knew that fifty dollars wouldn't buy much. He ordered a hot dog— the cheapest item on the menu—while Bo ordered a cheese- burger with extra french fries, a side of onion rings, a choc- olate shake, and an extra-large Coke. Then he ordered a New York strip and a Budweiser beer. "It's for my daddy to eat in the car," he said.

"Is that all, sweetie?" The waitress wore her hair in a high stack, and a pin on her blouse said BARB.

Their mother said no steak and no beer. She even tried to say it in Bo's language, which meant she was desperate. "Daddy isn't hungry for lunch. He's already eaten too many Cheez Whiz crackers."

Bo pulled a snub-nosed revolver from his trousers, where he always kept it, and slammed it down on the table. Benny had seen his little brother practice behavior like this at home in the bathroom mirror. He had picked it up from TV. "Daddy is too hungry," he said. He was whispering to make his anger seem more adult, just as men with guns sometimes did on programs like *The A Team* and *Knight Rider*.

"If that gun's not real," the waitress said, "it sure looks real." Benny saw the fear beginning in the woman's large blue eyes. "It's not real, is it?" There was nothing tinny, silvery, or counterfeit about it. It was black and heavy, like a real gun. Bo had picked it up in a toy store three days ago and began looking down its barrel, aiming it, making explosive noises as he pretended to shoot the people standing in line at the cash register. "You're dead! You're dead!" he kept saying. "That's a lot of toy gun you got there, son," the salesman had said. Their mother refused to buy it, but Bo screamed and hollered—as he did for everything he wanted these days—and finally aimed it at her face. "Buy it for me, Momma."

"It's just a stupid toy," Benny said now. "And you can't have the steak and the beer, Bo. We can't afford it."

The little boy slapped the tabletop with the gun again. "Yes I can," he said. "I can. I can."

Benny felt tired. He didn't want to fight with his little brother today. So the waitress walked away to get their food and to get the steak and beer for their father.

After lunch, they pulled up to a gas station, where they let Black out to run a little and stretch his legs. Instead, the dog walked to the side of the station and was sick against the yellow wall. Bo had let him eat the steak too quickly. Benny's mother tried to use her credit card. But the machine kept rejecting it and the small man with the brown face and the red baseball cap with MACK on it said, "Sorry, ma'am. I can't take it." She gave him cash, and Benny watched her count the remaining money—seven bucks. Even Benny knew that seven bucks was not a lot of money.

When they drove onto the highway again, the California desert opened up—a sky full of brush and burnt-out crust and earth in front of Benny and his family. Benny looked behind him, where the emptiness had just swallowed the little gas station. He wanted to see an end to the desert. But there was none.

When the boys woke up, they saw their mother outside feeding quarters into a single pay phone, its bright phone-color blue shining alone in the desert. The boys and Black climbed out of the car and Bo put his little finger through the bullet holes that had been shot into the metal guard around the phone. Somehow the phone had survived. A few yards behind it lay some collapsed white boards that Benny guessed were once an outhouse. A black-and-white sign, also bullet-riddled, stood before the wreckage. Bo read the largest word, sounding out the thick black bars of each let-ter—D-A-N-G-E-R. It was cold. Their breathing was white smoke in the air and they told their mother that they needed their coats. Still groggy, they walked to the side of the road, undid their pants, and slowly found their penises. Bo needed to go, but he couldn't. "It's too cold. It won't tinkle," he shouted.

After peeing, Benny left his little brother and walked over to his mother, leaning into her with a large, tired em-brace. Her skinny body was trembling. She was talking to his grandparents on the phone and her voice was small, like a little girl's. "It's big out here, Daddy," she said. "I think I might be lost."

Benny could make out some of his grandfather's words coming through the receiver above him. "Nonsense . . . you must know . . . that's ridiculous. . . ."

She couldn't tell him which state she was in. "I'm in the desert. That's all I know, Daddy." His grandfather said something about road signs and his mother said yes, she could see one sign. Only one.

"Well, read me the stupid sign, Jeannie." The old man had become irritated and began to shout and Benny could hear everything. "Go ahead and read it!"

" 'DANGER!' " she read. " 'No digging. Contaminated soil.' "

There was silence between them now.

"Damn it, Jeannie," his grandfather finally yelled. "One more try. All you need to do this time is find the sun. Look in the sky and tell me where the stupid sun is, all right?"

Benny and his mother looked up at the sky at the same time. "There is no sun," she said. Her body began to shake again and Benny moved away from her a little. "We're in the desert. The boys are cold and I forgot our bags at home. All they have is T-shirts and jeans. The sky's gray, Daddy. It's like metal. It doesn't tell me anything." Jeannie dropped the receiver then and began walking toward the Impala, while Benny stood looking at the black piece of plastic dangling and spinning at the end of its metal cord. The tiny voices of his grandparents called out his mother's name. "Jeannie! Jeannie! Pick up the phone, Jeannie!"

Benny wondered if he should pick it up. But he didn't want to. Instead, he looked over the road where Bo and Black were playing a game of fetch the ball. The ball was a warm sphere of neon red and Benny found his eyes following its spastic motion as it shot into the darkening air. A storm was moving in now. The ball's irregular bounce discouraged the dog's attempts to fix on it and hunt it down. The animal turned circles, toppled sideways, barked and growled at the quick neon color. Bo raced in all directions after it, screaming, *"Fetch! Fetch!"* Cold air blew across the slate-colored landscape while Benny struggled to follow the tiny glow of the ball. Infrequently, a car shot by on the small two-lane road. "Jeannie! Jeannie!" the dangling receiver shouted. Barbed sickles of lightning began to flash in the distance when Benny finally picked the phone up. "Hello."

"Jeannie?"

"No. It's Benny," Benny said.

"Get your mother back on the phone this minute," the old man said.

"She won't come."

"Benny?" It was his grandmother's voice now. It sounded disapproving and annoyed. "Did your mother get my letter and my check?" Benny had seen the check and read his grandmother's letter, which he found on the kitchen table. The letter said that his mother should go out and clean herself up. Get her hair done, buy herself clothes and makeup and whatever else she would need to keep her husband home if he ever came back. "It is just too bad you had to marry a man like Rex at the age of seventeen," his grandmother had written. "But we all reap what we sow. So let's just hope that Rex comes home, because you'll never find another one. Men can't be expected to love a divorced woman with two boys of her own."

"Yes," Benny said. "She got them."

"Well, did she go out and fix herself up? Does your mother look pretty now?"

"Yes. She's pretty now." But that was a lie. Benny knew that his mother had spent more than half of the check on the expensive toy gun for Bo. The rest went to buy gas and food for the trip they were taking now.

"Good," the old woman said. "You tell her I expect her to look her best when you all come in."

"Benny boy?" It was his grandfather again and he spoke with a sudden masculine enthusiasm. "You know where you are, don't you? You're not lost, are you?"

Benny was following the warm dot of red as it shot over the road and into a bush. The tone in the old man's voice wanted Benny to say yes. So he said, "Yes, Gramps, I know where we are."

"That a boy! Now Benny, I'm putting you in charge, all right? It's your job to get your little brother and your mother to Grandpa and Grandma's for Thanksgiving, you hear?" The phone clicked then and a woman's voice that sounded like a computer asked Benny for money. But he didn't have any and the phone went dead in his hand. When he looked up, he couldn't find the red ball anymore and he saw that everything had gone negative in the storm colors. His little brother's white skin glowed and the dog's black color went oily and solid.

"We got to find it," Bo said. He was on his hands and knees, digging in a bush.

"Get your little butt in this car, Bo," Benny's mother said. Her voice sounded cruel.

"I won't leave without my ball!" She had to drag him, kicking and screaming, and throw him into the backseat.

"It's just a stupid ball," Benny told his little brother in the car. But after driving more than an hour into the storm, Benny still felt the loneliness of the plastic toy lost back there.

———

After the storm, the clouds went pink and purple like burned flesh and the setting sun came out, throwing a violet, acidic light over the desert. Bo said, "Look! A rainbow." Benny held on to the door handle in the front seat. He had just looked at the speedometer. It said 120 mph. They were driving up and down hills, and at the top of each hill the desert seemed to triple itself. There were almost no cars. More than ten minutes ago, they had passed a green bus driving in the opposite direction, empty except for the driver. Then a purple Cadillac with a fat blond woman at the wheel whipped by them and was gone. Then nothing again. Now, as they reached the top of the next hill, Benny saw the glimmer of a car ahead of them. Sitting beside him, his mother was a purple color in the strange light. He heard his little brother talking to the dog in the backseat. "Is Black hungry again?" he asked. "Momma, me and Black are hungry. We want something to eat."

"We'll get something next time we stop."

Benny felt tired and didn't want to look at the endless twilight and the burning sky. But every time he curled up and closed his eyes, one of his mother's hands reached over to caress him. It didn't feel like a caress. The hand was cold and squeezed his face and the back of his neck too hard. She seemed to be holding on to him and her grip felt panicky. "Do you think we're on the right road, Momma?" he asked. "There're not many cars."

One side of the sky began to get dark and bruised and Bo said, "I don't want it to get dark."

She said, "I don't want to talk, Benny. You curl up and go to sleep."

They were getting closer to the car ahead of them now, and Bo, who had just spotted it, shouted, "A car! A car!"

Jeannie slowed down as they approached. It was a small Toyota with Nevada license plates. Bo's head shot into the front seat to get a good look at the driver. A bar of rainbow hovered over the Toyota's hood. Inside the car, the light was pink, and when the man driving turned to look at them, the gentle fire of that color seemed to be making him, forging him in front of them.

"It's Daddy!" Bo shouted. Their mother stayed beside the Toyota, squinting across at its driver. "See?" Bo said. "It's him. It's Daddy."

"The bastard," she said. "It is him." They drove out in front of him and Benny felt the scream and power of the Impala's engine rise into his belly in a wave of warm nausea. "It's him," the little boy said again. Benny's mother pulled up alongside the other car again and hit the brakes, flinging Bo into the front seat. His legs kicked at the dash as the Impala careened into the small white car, hit, and swung out wide to the left. Benny held on, watching the desert and the strange squashed colors of sunset wobble in his window. "What are you doing, Momma?" The sound of the impact had been dull and hollow. The Toyota swerved on and off the shoulder until the man finally recovered the little car and now tried to outdrive them. But they easily shot in front of him and squeezed him toward the edge of the road again. "Got you, you bastard!" Jeannie yelled. In the backseat, Black began whining and barking. Benny looked back at the man's face. It was screaming something mutely at the Toyota's windshield. It was skinny and afraid and maybe had his father's colors. But it wasn't his father. "Momma!" Benny shouted. She looked furious in the purple light.

"Shut up, Benny," she said. This time the Toyota wobbled, then shot off the shoulder into the desert, where it rolled once before halting in an orange cloud of dust.

When they got out of the Impala to meet him, he was on his knees in the dirt, looking at himself—his hands and arms. Then he looked at his hands again because they were bleeding. His gray suit pants were ripped up one of his legs to the knee and his blue blazer lay over a bush behind him. Little white cards spilled from its torn breast pocket and blew over the desert floor. When he finally stood himself up, he said, "What the . . ." The man's face hung loose and expressionless. He lifted his hands and showed Jeannie how they were gloved in blood. "Look what you did to me." His voice wasn't angry. It sounded puzzled. "It hurts," he said.

"We got you, Rex, and you're not getting away. You hear me?" Jeannie said.

"Yeah," he said. He was looking around, stumbling, swaying. "What did you call me?" He looked back down at his hands.

Benny felt sick and started backing away from the scene. The stranger's head was bleeding into his white shirt now. The man looked ignorant and weak. Benny didn't want to see him anymore. "Momma, let's go. Let's leave him here and go. It's someone else. It's not Daddy." The desert was big and he couldn't seem to get away from the wrecked Toyota, the man looking at his hands, the blood. He looked into the distance, where the light was coming from. But he couldn't look into it for long, because the desert was making a gory red mess of the sun as it sucked it down.

"Look at this," Benny's mother said. She pointed at shiny pots and pans and dozens of squares of carpet in all colors and shags, spread among the bushes. She found kitchen knives, bathroom tiles, hot pads, towels and bed linen, brand-new and wrapped in plastic. She began gathering the stuff and loading it into the trunk of the Impala. "Jesus, Rex, where'd you get all this beautiful stuff?" She held a set of kitchen knives up to the man. "It's beautiful, Rex."

"Rex?" he said. "Rex's not my name." He tried to say his name now. "Where's my name?" he asked. He turned around in the desert. One of the small white cards blew at his feet and he pointed at it blowing away again. "There's my name."

Benny chased it down and trapped it beneath his foot. It was black on white and he read it out slowly. HOMES AND LIVING. Then he read the man's name, which was not their father's. "It's not him, Momma," Benny said.

"Throw it away," Jeannie said. She was putting a vacuum cleaner into the trunk. "That's not who you are. I know who you are, Rex," she said.

Benny put the card with the man's name in his back pocket. "Don't take the vacuum cleaner, Momma," he said. "You can't take the vacuum cleaner. It's not ours." His mother didn't seem to hear him, so he turned and looked the other way now—into the darker half of the sky. But he could still see the shadows of the man, his mother and little brother. They were giant evening shadows that stretched across the road and on into the desert. Every motion of the dark forms seemed absurdly large and forceful. His mother's shadow was still loading the car up, lifting massive, vague objects that shook the shape of the Impala as she loaded them. It's too much, Benny thought, to be taking. These massive objects. She should put them back, leave them where they lay. He watched his little brother's shape lift the gun and say, "Put your hands up, Daddy. You're sitting next to Momma in the front seat." The man's shadow was the largest—a strange, wobbly tower.

"Okay," it said.

When Benny turned around again, he saw his mother pull the man's wallet from his blazer and dig out the cash. "You've been working, Rex." She was counting the money. "You've been working a lot." She sounded so happy.

The man was buckled into the front seat now and Bo was careful to keep his gun on him. "Where are we driving to?" the stranger asked.

"We're going to Mother's," Jeannie said. "We're going to have Thanksgiving at Mother and Daddy's—and you better hope they forgive you."

They stopped at a gas station with a minimart on the outskirts of a little town. Something was wrong with the man behind the counter, who could take their mother's money but couldn't seem to hear her when she asked what direction Montana was in. He had a speech impediment and seemed to be saying, "That way. That way." They bought a can opener and four cans of baked beans with plastic spoons, a six-pack of Coke, and a loaf of Wonder bread, which they never usually bought because you paid for the name, their mother said. But this was her special treat. Though the beans were cold, the boys were hungry and ate them quickly, dipping folded pieces of white bread into the black sauce and beans. They had forgotten to get something for Black, who whined from hunger. When it got dark and they had finished eating and felt full and tired, the moon came out and its bone-colored light fell into the car and made the man's face look chalky and dead. "Is he all right, Momma?" Benny asked.

"Daddy's a little tired. That's all," she said.

Benny's little brother was wide awake, alert, and holding

the gun to the sleeping man's head. "You can put your stupid gun away now," Benny said.

"No way," Bo said.

Every now and then the man would twitch and begin dreaming again out loud in his sleep. He kept saying the name Wanda. He seemed to be calling her.

Bo asked, "Momma, who's Wanda?"

Without answering, she pushed and nudged the man out of his dream. Once, she hit him hard enough on the shoulder to wake him. His eyes shot open and he began making frightened, whimpering sounds at the sight of his hands in the moonlight. The blood on them was dried and black and the broken fingers bent off in a way that made Benny's stomach feel hot and sick. The man kept whining, until Benny got into the front seat and covered the wounds up in the pair of white tube socks that he had just taken off his own feet. The stranger's hands looked like paws now— simplified by the stupid white socks. He was quiet and went back to sleep. When he woke again, he was shivering. His arms, his legs, his face wouldn't stay still. He said, "Please, I'm cold." Bo said he was cold, too. The moon had gone down and it was black and the world outside the car felt like winter. They stopped at a rest site, where Black and Bo got out to pee while Benny covered the man and his bloody shirt in piles of new sheets and blankets and a comforter he got from the trunk. The man's head seemed orphaned and small above the bulky pile of blankets. He looked at Benny. His face was still trembling. He said, "Water, please. Water."

Benny slammed the door, cutting the man's voice off, and walked into the parking lot, where he heard his mother talking to an old man in a cowboy hat who was looking at the stars and saying their names out. "That there's the pole-star. See it, lady? And there's the Big and Little Dipper. Orion's over there." Benny began to feel dizzy with staring at the sky and trying to see names in the cold dust.

His mother said, "Mister, could you tell me where I am?"

He said, "Where you are?"

"What state I'm in."

"You're in Utah, lady."

She said, "Oh. That's not really where I wanted to be."

The man seemed offended. "Utah's a beautiful state, lady."

There was silence between them.

"Maybe you could help me," Jeannie said. "I got to find a beauty parlor first thing in the morning."

The man asked her, "A what?" and she told him again. "Well," he said, "there's beauty parlors in Utah. You bet there is." But he didn't seem to want to talk to her anymore and returned to the stars.

On the road again, Benny fed the stranger water from an empty Coke can he had filled in the rest room. He drank all the water and still said, *"Thirsty, thirsty, thirsty."* The stranger woke up several times in the night, speaking odd words and phrases and names of people Benny had never met. Before morning, when the dark outside was hollow and blue, Bo woke and wanted his daddy to speak with him. He put the gun to the man's head and said, "Say something to me, Daddy." The man said something, repeating it several times. It was barely audible, and Benny and Bo at first thought he was saying, "I'm your friend. I'm your friend." But it soon became clear to them that he was saying, "I'm afraid. I'm afraid." Then it was morning and the sun burned at the desert's edges until the cold yellow day was above them again. The man woke and could no longer speak. Benny was in front, working a sort of head bandage out of napkins for the stranger's wound. He had to hold the man's head to keep it still and could smell the stranger's exhaustion and the stranger's blood, which were warm smells. But they were cooling down, getting cold now. The napkins didn't work. They made the man's head look white and papery, too fragile to be fixed. "Momma," Benny said, "this isn't Daddy. You know this isn't Daddy." He put the stranger's head down again and it fell off the seat rest and leaned over the bloody glass of the side window. "We've got to go to the hospital, Momma."

They came into a small town, driving too fast. When they turned corners, the deadweight of the man's head rose and smacked the glass. "Momma," Benny said, "find a hospital, please." She was looking for something. When she found it, she pulled over and told Benny to come with her and for Bo to watch Daddy and Black in the car. She sounded exhilarated and frantic. "This is going to work for us, boys. After I'm done, Daddy's never leaving us again." She counted the bundle of money, pocketed it, then walked Benny into the beauty parlor, holding his hand tightly enough to make the joints in his fingers crack and hurt.

The shop was a bright pink color inside and stank of hair sprays, perfumes, things acidic and barely breathable, of suds and warm water and of the stiff hair of two old ladies who sat under large jug-shaped dryers, each reading a magazine as the machines worked on them. Bright yellow lightbulbs surrounded all the mirrors and long fluorescent cathode tubes buzzed white light down from the ceiling. There were no shadows in the room, and all the objects— the barber's chairs, the bottles and tubes of soap, Benny, his mother, the two old ladies, and the magazines they read— were doubled, tripled, multiplied in the mirrors. Benny was glad to be holding his mother's hand now, because he felt dizzy in this bright circus of images. The only hole in it was the glass door of the entrance, through which Benny could see Bo sitting in the car with the handgun to the stranger's head.

The hairdresser entered the room through a curtain in the back. She was a huge woman, wearing a purple-colored barber's coat. Her hair was high and long, the same color of reddish purple as her coat. Her makeup looked fresh, still wet on her face. She said, "Come over here, honey." She sat Benny's mother down in one of the pink thrones and he sat behind them. His mother's eyes filled with tears at the sight of her dirty face and the dry mess of her hair. The hairdresser handed her some tissues and said, "We're gonna polish you up, honey. Don't you worry. You're gonna feel better." She lowered his mother's head into the sink now, shampooed her and soaped her face. The large woman was looking at Benny. "Your boy have a nosebleed or something? It's amazing how much boys can bleed. Mine scrape their knees, cut themselves, hit their heads. Bleed and bleed. Nothing hurts them."

She left for a minute to release the old women from the dryers. One of them was waving a bony hand at Benny and he felt himself waving back. "So cute," the old woman said. They paid and hobbled off, looking behind them at Benny and his mother.

Then the large woman was standing in front of Benny with a steaming washcloth in her hands. The cloth was incredibly white. "Put your arms out, sweetie," she said. It was hard to breathe in the woman's perfume, and her beauty—her large hair and painted face—seemed too bright, electric, almost dangerous. But the hairdresser's plump hands were forceful and warm as they squeezed his fingers. One of them gripped his shoulder and she wiped

his face in the warm cloth. "That feels better, doesn't it?"
It did.

Benny was looking at the large posters of beautiful
women taped to the mirrored wall in front of him—women
with blond hair like wings or with roped and braided hair.
Their faces were new and smooth and cosmetic. Some of
them had men holding on to them. "You like them?" the
woman asked. She wet his hair and combed it back twice.
She laughed. "Ready for church." The cloth in her hands
was soggy and red with blood now.

He said yes. He did like them.

"We're gonna make your momma just as pretty as that."
Benny watched as the woman clipped his mother's hair
down, cut and combed and arranged it. The blow-dryer was
a tubular white handgun that made his mother's hair fluff
into feathery crests. The beauty was happening to his
mother now. It was a fragile, warm-looking sheath of fluo-
rescence surrounding her head. "You looking forward to
turkey day tomorrow?" she asked Benny. The woman re-
clined the pink seat a little to do his mother's makeup. The
instruments she used were sharp little brushes, barbed and
strange. She said the colors out loud as she applied them.
"Now some turquoise around the eyes, with some dusky
purple at the edges. We're giving you the soft evening look,
all right, hon? The right colors for autumn. That's what
I've got on today. I think you'll like it."

When she sat Benny's mother up again, he saw that the
hairdresser and his mother had the same face now. It was
a pretty face, but not his mother's. The face was hurt and
angry around the eyes, which were tender and purple.
"You like it?" the woman asked him. He nodded. "Well
then, tell her you do, sweetie," she said. "I don't think
any of them know what we need." She was speaking to his

mother. "You got to tell us some nice things sometimes, sweetie."

He said, "I like it." He hoped that neither woman heard the fear in his voice.

When Benny and his mother walked out of the beauty parlor, a gray sky was pushing down on the little town. Black was lifting his leg on parking meters at the end of the street, and Benny wanted to know why the dog was loose. He knocked on Bo's car window and felt a warm pissy smell hit his face when Bo rolled the window down. The little boy had put his gun away. "Black peed in here. I had to let him out so he wouldn't pee anymore. It wasn't his fault." Bo seemed tired and his voice was small and weak. "Don't you hurt him, Benny. It wasn't his fault. He doesn't need to be punished."

Since their father had left, Benny was the only one ever to punish the stupid animal when it needed it. "The car's not the place for the dog to pee, Bo." He went after it, calling its name. The animal must have heard the anger in his voice, because it was dodgy and tried to elude Benny's hand when he grabbed it by the collar. The dog's mouth let out a stinky smoke of breath in the cold air and its wet eyes begged for mercy. It was Bo's dirty animal—spoiled, no good anymore. Bo had fed it so much people food that it wouldn't eat its own dry dog food now. It slept in Bo's bed with him and lounged on the old couch in their living room and didn't even know it was a dog. It thought it was human, and its wet eyes were saying that to Benny now. I'm like you. I'm like you, they said. He hit the animal three times with the palm of his hand, then let it go. It tried to come back twice, wagging and penitent, but Benny kicked at it until it ran down the street and stayed away.

When he got back to the car, he saw a group of men gathering on the other side of the street, talking and looking at the blue Impala. Inside the car, his mother was holding the man's head in her hands. It was the first time she had touched him. Benny closed himself into the pissy stink of the Impala. "Daddy doesn't talk or move or anything anymore," Bo told him.

"Shut up," Jeannie said. She held the man's face directly to hers. "Open your eyes, Rex."

She wasn't careful where she put her hands. Benny wished that she would be more careful, because the way she was holding him must have hurt him. "Look at me, Rex," she said. When the man's eyes didn't open, she opened them with her thumbs, but they didn't seem to see her. "Rex, damn it! Here I am." She was whispering.

"How come you didn't bring Black back?" Bo asked.

"He won't come."

"We got to get him," Bo said.

Their mother let the man's head drop against the glass and lifted her hands. There was blood on them.

"He won't come," Benny said. "He doesn't want to come."

"We got to get him anyway."

But something was happening outside now. The sheriff's car had pulled up and a man knocked on their window. He said something about an ambulance not coming today. There had been a bad accident on the interstate and all the ambulances were out. They should follow him. He said the word *hospital.* So they followed the red lights of the sheriff's car. After they turned the corner, Bo looked back to see Black running after them in the distance. "We forgot Black. We got to stop for Black." They drove and followed the sheriff's car, until the dog disappeared behind them and Benny had to pin the little boy to his seat.

"Forget Black," he said.

At the hospital, the light was yellow and closed in with pain and hurt people. Benny heard two men talking about the accident—something about cars and a station wagon, ice and danger on the roads—and everything was too bad, just too bad, they said. An old woman fell over in the hall-way. Benny looked around, but nobody explained it to him. People were traveling fast on beds with wheels. He thought maybe he should be looking for someone. A nurse was in his face, telling him and Bo to sit on the floor and stay there. He looked behind him. Two little blond girls were playing with a doll in a corner. They took turns loving it and gave it a beautiful girl name—a flower name—Lilly or Rose or Violet. They were the only ones that the pain in the hospital did not seem to be calling to. "Everything's going to be okay," they told the doll. Benny resisted the urge of ripping the toy away and making them scream for it. The nurse was still telling him to sit. But when Bo slipped past her, she went after him, and Benny was free to move again.

He moved until a woman seized him. She was crying hard, her eyes sudden and shocking, like broken glass. She embraced Benny until his face hurt, pressing against her bones. A man worked his hands between him and the woman and wrenched them apart. "He's not ours," the man said. "He's someone else's."

The nurse came back again, angry. Bo was still loose, and she didn't seem to care about keeping Benny in his seat now. He saw a toy car roll through the crowded feet over the floor and on into the next room. He followed it, wondering when the child who had pushed it would come. He looked around him, but no child came. The car was a bright red color that burned against the white of the walls. It was kicked around until it disappeared in the crowded stomp of feet. He saw two policemen questioning his mother in the far corner. She was crying her soft-evening face off into tissues and dropping it at her feet. The officers said, "The man in your car was dead on arrival. Can you give us his name? We don't think he's your husband, lady, and we have to ask you about the goods in your trunk." Benny reached into his back pocket and felt the soft paper on which the man's name was printed.

He found Bo in another room. Bo was looking at a scream through the crack in a curtain. The scream sounded like the noise an animal would make. Benny looked through the crack now over his little brother's shoulder. He saw a small family—a man and a woman holding a boy's hands. The boy was lying on his back. Benny couldn't make much of him out. The scream died. Then the boy kicked his legs and it began again. The doctor was pulling a red thread up and down over the boy's face. He seemed happy. "All done," he said. "We're all done."

The woman and man kept holding the boy. They said, "Everything's going to be okay."

"Are those two yours?" the doctor asked, pointing at Benny and Bo.

The man and the woman looked up at them. They were young and pleasant-looking. "No. We don't know them."

"Out of here, boys," the doctor said. "Scat."

Benny backed off, but Bo didn't. Bo swung the curtain wide open, unhitched his gun, and bandied it in the doctor's face. The man and the woman fell back and the boy sat up—a little boy, smaller even than Bo. He was naked above the waist, and Benny saw the delicate bones below his neck. His eyes were groggy, tired of so much pain. "Don't," Benny said.

But Bo's face was a hard, furious mask. He cocked the revolver. "Hey!" he shouted at the boy. "You're dead!"

The ring of the blanks shut off the sound of pain in the hospital. The fluorescent tubes buzzed in their sockets and a curl of smoke drifted upward from the snub-nosed barrel of Bo's gun. "It's a silly toy gun," a man's voice said. When the hospital learned that, the pain came alive again and Bo flung his gun away and put his hands in the air.

"Stupid gun," Bo shouted. A large man clothed in white picked Bo up from his middle and carried him away, kicking and screaming.

When the same man returned, Benny held his hand out with the crumpled card. "It's him," Benny said. "It's the man."

"What man?" he said.

"We've done some bad things," Benny said. "My mother and brother and me."

"Sure you have," he said. He took the card from Benny, wadded it up, and threw it into a garbage bin as they walked out of the room.

That day, Benny and his little brother were driven in the back of a police car to a large house with a green front yard and a fenced-in backyard with trees and a swing set. The inside of the police car was black and had the cold smell of bullets and real guns. There was a cage between the boys in back and the policemen in front. Benny's little brother clung to the cage, snarling, barking, showing his teeth. The men laughed and called Bo Rover. "There are some real crazies out there," they said. "You just can't believe what some crazies will do." One of them turned around and looked at Benny and said, "It's a lucky thing you and your little brother, the dog, weren't killed back there. You know that? If I had been there," he said, "I woulda shot both of you."

The house belonged to a man and his wife. They were called the Greens. If you wanted them to hear you, you had to call them Mr. and Mrs. Green. That was the rule. There were other boys in the house, too, and you had to get along with them. That was another rule. Benny wanted his little brother to behave and follow the rules, but he wouldn't. Bo barked and growled, and Mr. Green, a thick man who smelled like a car garage and metal tools, laughed at first. He said he thought little boys were humans and should act that way. Mr. Green patted Benny on the back and called him a good boy. He said, "I know you've seen some bad things, Benny. But you're a good boy."

The next day was Thanksgiving. The sun came out and thick, shaggy rays of light covered the huge dinner table and made the cooked turkey, the sweet potatoes and broccoli, and Mr. and Mrs. Green shine. Mr. and Mrs. Green looked very thankful for everything. While Mr. Green prayed, Bo growled. Another boy at the table wore a naked Barbie doll chained to his belt buckle. He popped the doll's pretty blond head off and put it on the table beside his plate. When Bo would only eat his dinner with his face in the food, Mr. Green picked him up by his pants and held him in the air. "If you act like a dog, we'll treat you like a dog." He sent him from the table.

Later that night, Bo was furious at the boy with the Barbie doll chained to his belt and bit him, drawing blood where the teeth marks were on his arm. For that, Bo had to sleep alone in the little room in the roof of the house.

Benny didn't want his little brother to be a dog. All the same, he dreamed that night about the dog in the dog movie that he hated and Bo loved so much. He dreamed of Bo's favorite scene, when the dog drives his father's car without asking. It was a longhaired, shaggy dog and the car was a large glossy sedan, more beautiful than any car Benny had ever driven in. The animal sat upright, one paw resting on the wheel, while the other, furry and strange, hung out the open window. A light breeze blew in the animal's coat and its eyes moved with a great sensitivity to the streets and the laws of the streets, soft, calm, knowing eyes, filled with the human act of driving. Benny knew that Bo was right. The dog was a better driver than their mother. Their mother had been a horrible driver, the worst driver.

In the morning, when it was still dark and no one in the house was awake, Benny went up to the room in the roof and got into the small bed with Bo. His brother had refused to wash or clean himself at all. He smelled salty, humid, warm. Benny drew himself close, curling into the little human animal and wanting the morning to be dark and the day and the light of day never to come, so that he could stay there next to his little brother, the dog, forever.

OUTLAWS

At the beginning of winter, not long after Gary's fifteenth birthday, his father, William, fell from a ski lift. William had been drinking from minibottles of scotch and smoking dope at the time. William had never been a big drinker. He had made record sales as a furniture salesman that year and had gone up the mountain to celebrate with Howard, William's closest friend. It was Howard who was the big drinker and smoker. It was Howard who had brought the scotch and dope along. Evidently, the height from which William fell should not have been a fatal height. But he fell the wrong way—at a precise and extremely unlikely angle. The world, Gary thought, must have been working against his father. The sky, the clouds, the rocks—nothing was innocent.

At the funeral, Gary and his mother, Barbara, huddled together at the back of the room. Barbara's parents were both dead and she had only a few surviving relatives, none of whom were able to attend the services. Barbara wept and said, "Something good is going to happen to us soon. I know it will." Because they had rarely gone to church, their Presbyterian minister—a man whose voice was oddly small in comparison to his bulk—did not recognize them, though he spoke about William as if he had known him pleasantly for years and described him as a humble man of quiet integrity. Gary found none of these banalities at all comforting.

Howard had come to the funeral and tried to approach them after the sermon. But he was obviously drunk and afraid and he circled back. Dianne, his ex-wife, held him up and said a little too loudly, "We need to go talk to them, Howard." Dianne was a determined, wiry woman, and an extremely successful real-estate agent. She and Howard had been divorced for seven years, but they maintained what Gary's father had called "a moody, habitual friendship." Howard wore a black tuxedo, the collar and jacket of which Dianne repeatedly adjusted for him. Gary didn't want to have to talk to these two. But they finally came around again and faced Gary and his mother. "We're very sorry," Dianne said.

Howard opened his mouth. He smelled of hair tonic and liquor. "I don't know what to say," he said.

Barbara looked up at him. "As far as we're concerned," she said, "you did this to him."

During the winter months after William's death, Gary's mother took a leave of absence from the school where she worked as a speech therapist, and neither she nor Gary left the house or each other. They couldn't easily remain alone in a room or close doors behind them. Barbara roamed through the house in her terry-cloth robe, which was sometimes half-open, so that her underwear showed. These glimpses of his mother startled Gary. He was seeing something raw and unprotected in her. They ate with their fingers from paper plates. They didn't do laundry. They didn't clean or bathe often enough. They didn't answer the phone.

They didn't open mail or shovel snow. They let the winter cover their walks, their driveway, their green Buick. They let it erase things.

Gary tried to comfort his mother. He touched her back and shoulders when she wept. It was scary to give this sort of touch—the sort of touch that adults gave children— reliable and protective, as if he really had this strength. He drew baths for her, put perfumed bubbles in the water, stood outside the closed bathroom door and talked to her while she bathed. "I feel like leftovers," she said once. Gary wasn't sure what she meant and didn't want to know. He guessed that she had looked at herself in there—her nakedness, her aloneness—and hadn't liked what she saw. "Clean, clean, clean," he said through the door, in a happy voice that Barbara did not respond to. Her sadness seemed far more dangerous than his own, and when she began to weep in the tub, when she said to herself, "Oh God, look at me," he walked quietly away from his station outside the door and left her alone with her grief.

Gary had his own grief to attend to. His dead father seemed to be everywhere in the house. He was in the laundry in Barbara's closet—a heavy, twisted pile with the faint odor of something barely alive, barely festering. He was in the bathroom cabinet—shaving cream, razors, a worn bar of white hand soap sunk in the quagmire of the soap dish, where a few of his curled pubic hairs floated. He was in a family portrait taken last year and sitting on the fireplace mantel in the living room—a pale, pear-shaped man with a soft, malleable face and wet eyes. His body had become increasingly muffinlike, William himself had said, as he advanced into his late thirties. There had been nothing indomitable, defiant, or heroic about him. Nothing in him had seemed to deserve or provoke death.

The strangest remnant of William was a red party balloon that William had inflated and given to Gary as a sort of joke for his fifteenth birthday because Gary had outgrown balloons. William's sense of humor had been peculiar, but well meaning. The balloon said HAPPY BIRTHDAY on it. Gary stared through the stretched membrane at the invisible breath of his dead father. He considered pricking it. But that seemed wrong. So he shoved the balloon under his bed and hoped that it could get lost there.

Three weeks after William's death, Gary loaded the pile of dirty laundry—it had a distinct, almost sweet smell by then—into a basket and walked a mile and a half in the white January afternoon to a Laundromat called Wash-O-Rama. Inside Wash-O-Rama, the walls were an aqua-green color and the air smelled of dirty socks and detergent and of the babies and toddlers who sat in strollers or lay across the tables on which their mothers folded and sorted wash.

When Gary lifted the wet ropes of his laundry from the washing machine, his father's clothes were almost beyond recognition. He had washed the whites with the darks and the colors had bled. The drying part of the process seemed less complicated, but Gary felt awkward and self-conscious as he tried to fold one of his mother's bras.

"Not like that." This came from a girl, about his age, who sat on the hood of a working dryer, her legs crossed at the ankles. Behind her ankles, several pairs of lavender-and-citrus-colored panties churned in the round hatchlike window of the machine. "Like this." She made a complicated folding gesture with her hands that Gary couldn't quite follow. "Here," she said. She crossed over to him and folded the bra herself, oddly at ease with his mother's underwear in hand. "The cups fold into each other like that. See?"

She looked at his pile and said, "Oops. Looks like you fucked up. There's a chemistry to laundry, you know." She sounded superior, but kind. Her hair was dark and her eyes were a muddy color of brown, so soft they seemed to smear. She wore an achingly purple jewel—its color bristled in the white light of that place—pierced in her nose. Gary recognized her from school, where she hung out with a different, harsher set of kids. Gary didn't really hang out at all. He was a quiet type.

She put down the bra. "I'm Vickie," she said. "I've seen you around."

Gary didn't say his name. He had just lifted a wool sweater—it had been William's—out of the pile. The sweater had shrunk in the dryer to about Gary's size, and the thought that his dead father's sweater would now fit him was terrible and repulsive to Gary.

"It's a weird color," Vickie said. It had been a charcoal color, but was now a strange vascular shade of red.

"I don't like it anymore," Gary said. The suggestion that it had been his was, of course, a lie. But the truth of the sweater seemed too obscene to tell. "You want it?"

"Sure," she said. "It's sort of different." She put it on over her T-shirt and modeled it in the reflective glass of the Laundromat windows. She seemed happy with it. It suits her, Gary thought. "I sort of like it," she said. "Thanks."

In the middle of February, casseroles began to appear on Gary and Barbara's front porch. The doorbell would ring and there they were—in glass dishes, covered with foil. Gary dished out a helping for himself and a helping for

Barbara. "Come on, Mother," he said. "You've got to eat." Gary was determined that his mother would eat. He was determined that she would bathe and groom and dress. This new mode of his made him feel strange, not quite himself. Sometimes he faced his reflection in the mirror, an exercise that clarified nothing except that his acne had thickened a little. Sometimes he said "Fifteen . . . fifteen" to the mirror, trying to make the connection between himself and his age, because lately he had been feeling much older. He put a fork in Barbara's hand. "Eat," he said. "Eat." He had mastered a certain angry but affectionate voice that worked on his mother, and she ate.

The casseroles weren't exactly delicious—some lacked salt and pepper; others were undercooked or burned and nearly inedible—but they were small miracles of much-needed food. Gary suspected Vickie of cooking them. Vickie had been easy to get to know. She worked at a 7-Eleven in Gary's neighborhood, where Gary would spend his nights talking to her. "Not that I wouldn't," she told him. "But I couldn't cook a hole in the ground." Vickie had a lot of sayings that weren't really sayings and didn't make a lot of sense, but that you remembered anyway. Later on in February, buckets from Kentucky Fried Chicken, pizzas, and cartons of Chinese takeout replaced the casseroles. Whoever was showing this charity had given up on cooking.

Gary took Vickie home with him one afternoon and tried to introduce her to Barbara. But Barbara walked into her room and stayed there. Vickie had a distinctive, fluttering laugh, and she didn't need much of an excuse to use it. Her laugh had a surprising, chaotic range, almost purposeful, almost musical. After a while, Gary's mother said from behind the door, "Would you please tell your friend that I'm not feeling well, that we can't have guests right now."

So Gary and Vickie went to a coffeehouse called Alters—
they had been spending a lot of time there lately—where
college kids lounged around on fat armchairs and couches.
Vickie was teaching Gary to drink his coffee black. "It's
cheaper that way," she said. "All that funny, sweet milky
shit costs." Vickie was also teaching him to smoke. She said,
"I don't care what you say about your health and cancer
and all that. If you've got a cigarette in your hands, the
camera's on you." He probably shouldn't have been trying
out these new, bad habits. The curiosity didn't seem proper,
not at this time anyway. But Gary was young and hadn't
done much yet and Vickie was gleeful, transgressive, and
kind of sexy. She had taken to his father's sweater. She wore
it three or four times a week now, and it continued to look
good on her.

The sun came out that afternoon. In the middle of winter,
there it was, bulbous and artificial-looking. In Alters, the
college kids squinted in the brightness, and a large slab of
light—buzzing with molecular dust—lay over Gary and
Vickie. Vickie said, "Cool. It's like the world is trying to
say something." Then she said, "I'm sorry. I was laughing
in your house. I don't think your mom wanted laughter in
her house. I can't imagine it—someone just being dead like
that." When Gary didn't say anything, she said, "Hey,
where are you?"

Gary was thinking about Barbara, trying not to resent
her for what she had just done. "Oh, I'm here," he finally
said.

Vickie and Gary touched fingertips, setting off static
sparks as sharp as little teeth. Their open hands touching
made a shadow on the wall like scaffolding—a small skel-
etal shelter. Gary had felt a compulsion toward the truth
lately and he needed to tell Vickie a small truth now. "That

sweater you're wearing was never mine," he said, fingering its red cuff. "It was his—my father's."

"Oh God," she said, starting to remove it. "I can't take it. Not if it's his."

"Please," Gary said. "I don't want it to be his anymore. I don't want him to own anything anymore. Please keep it."

On a Thursday afternoon, at about the time the anonymous food would arrive, the doorbell rang, and Howard—the man who had skied with Gary's father that day—stood on the porch holding two white bags from Taco Bell. "I've been a coward," Howard said. "I need to tell you that it's me. I'm the food guy."

Although Howard had been William's best friend, Gary's mother had never liked him much. Howard was what she called "party-happy." He was a darester, a sort of domestic stuntman, who'd always brought out a little of the same male bravado in William, otherwise a quiet man. William had kept Howard as a friend—or at least this was Barbara's theory—because Howard was a version of William's fantasy self. If William could have been two men, he would have been the stable man who lived with his wife and son, and then he would have been Howard.

Howard tried to put the bags of food in Gary's hands, but Gary made no effort to take them. Howard's shirt was wrinkled and his face was pale and bruised around the eyes from sleeplessness. He smelled vaguely of bedsheets, and Gary wondered how Howard could be anyone's fantasy self.

"How were my casseroles?" Howard asked.

"Bland," Gary said. He felt suddenly fierce toward Howard.

"I know I can't cook worth shit," Howard said. He sounded sad. "That's not one of the things I do."

"Who's there?" Barbara asked from somewhere inside the house. Gary told her and she said, loudly enough for Howard to hear it, "Tell him to go away."

Gary said, "Go away." When Howard didn't go, Gary said, "Please."

In the last week of February, the weather turned unusually warm for Utah. Winds blew in from the south and it rained and the muggy smell of mud filled the air. Swarms of gnats were born in the gray afternoons. The snow in the mountains melted and ski resorts reported huge losses. Let them lose money, Gary thought. Let them lose all the money in the world.

At night, Gary would walk the two blocks from his house to the 7-Eleven where Vickie worked. Water flowed in the gutters and Gary felt something loosening inside him and seeping away.

That night, Gary found Vickie working the 7-Eleven alone. The night manager, a tall, pale, skinny man named Abbott, sometimes let her work the shop on slow nights while he'd go over to Melissa's, his girlfriend's, and, or so Vickie claimed, nibble on her toes until midnight, when he would return for the graveyard shift. "I'd like to do it with you sometime," Vickie said from behind the counter at the 7-Eleven. She looked at him with an adult confidence in her eyes.

"Do it?" Gary asked.

"You know," she said. "Fuck." Gary could hardly believe she had used that word, though it hadn't sounded at all derogatory in her mouth. It sounded playful, good-humored.

"That's all right," Gary said.

Vickie and he were eating cookies from an open box of

Chips Ahoy. Vickie ate whole cookies in one bite. She fed one to Gary, caressed the crumbs from his chin, and said, "We didn't pay for these, you know. We're stealing. We're outlaws. How does it feel to be an outlaw?"

"Worrying," Gary said. He imagined Abbott coming back from Melissa's any minute and catching them with the open box of cookies. He felt a rush of guilt and shame. He was no good at small crimes.

"Don't worry," Vickie said, feeding him another cookie. "I know what to do to make it safe. I know what to use and all that." Then, after he had chewed and swallowed his cookie, she said, "What's the matter? You scared of it?"

"Scared of what?"

"Fucking," she said.

Gary was surprised again by that word—how gentle it could sound—and saw no reason why he shouldn't be absolutely honest. There was something about Vickie that wanted the truth from him again and again. "Sort of." Then, after a pause, he said, "Very scared, I guess."

One night something horrible and unexpected almost happened. Gary had been about to open the glass door of the 7-Eleven, when he saw a man pointing a handgun at Vickie's face. Gary heard the robber repeat the word *bitch*. The gun in his hand had that dark, monstrous quality of genuine danger about it. Black metal was a terrible thing. Gary did not have to deliberate. He walked in the front door and stood there.

"What the fuck are you doing?" the robber said.

"I'm her friend," Gary said. "I'm not going to do anything. I just don't want her to be alone."

"Take your goddamn hands out of your pockets, then," the robber commanded. Gary did this. The robber's face looked like a pale vegetable—cool and raw—beneath the brown panty hose. He looked like any robber Gary had seen on television, except that he was trembling. He seemed afraid of the thing he was doing, and this fear was the real quality about him.

Vickie kept saying, "Look, I don't care about this place. You can take whatever you want."

Gary had the same thought: Take it all.

Gary thought that this moment was maybe one of the reasons William had gone. William's death had allowed Gary to walk into the store that night. William's death was the terrible thing that made every other terrible thing more likely and less terrible.

The robber took the cash in the register—two twenty-dollar bills, some ones, and a few rolls of coins—a pocketful of king-size Snickers bars, a liter of Diet Coke, and nothing else. "Are you sure that's all he took?" Abbott asked, walking in only minutes after the robber had left. "Lucky," he said. "That's all I can say. You kids are lucky." It was true: It did seem like a generous act of robbery, so generous that when the police arrived, Vickie and Gary constructed a story. They said their robber had driven a blue Ford van, when, in fact, he had driven a VW Bug the gray color of rain. They said he had been a Mexican or Cuban or something like that, when, in fact, he had been a skinny, balding white guy. They wanted their robber to go free. They wanted him to be an event that happened to them and then disappeared into the night. They wanted to keep this thing. It was their secret and they had survived it.

At the beginning of March, Gary woke one morning to see Barbara carrying bags of groceries into the house. "You went to the store?" Gary asked.

"Citrus," she said, "is so god-awful expensive in the winter months."

"You went to the store?" Gary asked again.

She looked slightly embarrassed now, as if she suddenly realized who had been in control of the household all this time. "Yes," she said. Her hair wasn't done. Her face looked raw and weepy and the zipper on her pants was half-open. But there she stood with a bag of oranges and grapefruits so heavy, she needed both arms to hold it up. "I invited Howard and Dianne over for dinner tonight," she said. "If you want, you can invite your little friend, too. I think we need people again." That word *little*—"little friend"—was his mother speaking. It was her old adult way of seeing his younger world as harmless and diminutive.

He wanted to tell her about her zipper. But he wasn't sure he could take care of her now. She was piling fruit into the fridge and looked strong. He said, "Vickie's her name."

"That's a nice name," she said.

"You might not like her. She's kind of bad. She's a rebel."

"If you like her," Barbara said, "I like her." That was his mother, too—this stern resistance to disagreement.

"Maybe," Gary said.

That evening, Vickie wore a T-shirt that said GIRLS KICK ASS on the front, and Howard said, "So is that supposed to be a feminist remark? Is it supposed to mean freedom or something?" Howard asked these questions in a tone of honest curiosity.

"No," Vickie said. "I don't think so. It's just supposed to mean what it says. What do you do to make money?" she asked. Vickie and Howard were trying to have a normal conversation. They were trying to take each other seriously, and it seemed to be working.

"I sell paper bags and plastic sacks."

"He's got this bumper sticker on his Lincoln," Dianne added, "that says, 'I have sacks appeal.'" They all laughed at this. It seemed funny to them, despite the obvious fact that it wasn't.

Dianne talked about selling houses, because she had just signed the papers on a house that afternoon. She seemed to like Vickie, though she obviously wasn't accustomed to dealing with young people. "So is this your girlfriend, Gary? Are you two going steady?" Dianne asked.

Gary didn't know what to say, so Vickie answered for him. "Sure," she said. "But that word's not really used anymore. I guess you would say that we're together."

Before dinner started, Vickie went up to Barbara and whispered in her ear. Barbara blushed and laughed, then fastened her zipper. Gary was grateful for this woman-to-woman gesture. It seemed easy for all of them to gather here.

Howard looked self-consciously washed. He gave off an odor of aftershave and his clothes smelled like too much laundry soap. Barbara cooked chicken breasts with a sauce made from combining canned cream of mushroom soup and white wine. She wore her baby blue cardigan, though the buttons weren't properly aligned. Evidently, her grief was still beyond buttons and zippers. "I thought we should feed *you* for once," Barbara said to Howard. His food had kept coming all through February and on into March. Every afternoon, the pizza or burgers or chicken appeared. It was hard to ignore the person who fed you. It was hard for Gary and Barbara to keep thinking poorly of him.

After they cleaned their plates, Howard and Dianne kept saying to Barbara, "You look good. You really do."

"Nonsense," Barbara said. "I look stricken."

Everyone at the table denied this, even though it was true.

When they finished eating their ice cream, Barbara looked at Howard. "Will you tell us something? Will you tell us what he said just before it happened?"

Earlier that night, Howard had discovered two six-packs of William's beer in the fridge and had helped himself. "Just one or two," he had said. After his fifth beer, he became mournful and vulnerable. "Please, let's not think about that now," he said.

"You're making a baby out of yourself, Howard," Dianne said. "Don't get infantile on us."

"He didn't really say anything," Howard said. "I wasn't looking at him at the time. I was looking down at my skis. I saw the little K2 insignia on the tips. Then he made a sort of sighing sound. I'm sorry, but I don't think I could make that sound for you now. When I looked over at him, he was already gone."

Outside it rained. Gary thought the rain was repetitive and similar to all rain that had ever fallen. Howard drank another beer or two and seemed to forget everyone else and wept. To his relief, Gary was able to pity him without disliking him. Just before Howard and Dianne walked out the door, Howard held on to the door frame and said, "I'm sorry. I'm sorry."

Barbara said, "It's okay, Howard," and she seemed to mean it.

In March the world froze again. The air turned chalky and cruel, though the sun shone, so that the cold was bright and electric, like the inside of a freezer, everything stubbled and crystallized. Barbara walked through the house with intent now, her robe closed tightly around her. She went back to her job as a speech therapist, where she taught kids with impediments how to speak—how to be a part of a community of language and sound. Howard and Dianne came to dinner once or twice a week. Howard was quiet and more contemplative than he had ever been. Barbara didn't allow him to drink in her house now. That was the rule, and Howard obeyed it.

One afternoon, when Gary and Vickie were on Gary's bed "trying things out"—this was what Vickie called it— Vickie discovered the balloon beneath his bed. They had been "trying things out" for a while now, though this time they had gone the furthest. Vickie sat astride him and put Gary's hands on her breasts. "Kiss them," she said. Vickie was very unafraid to say things. "Kiss them worshipfully." Gary didn't know what a worshipful kiss was, but she seemed to like his kisses anyway. She opened her mouth and made the sounds of pleasure Gary recognized from movies he had seen. He tasted a mix of salt and perfumed soap as he kissed her. "Relax," she said. "The whole world does this." Nonetheless, Gary tried not to think of the whole world. She was doing something pleasant to him with her hands. Then they sort of bounced around, until Gary wasn't sure what was happening and lost courage. Vickie wasn't worried. The first time doing anything was stranger than you thought it would be, she said. "We'll get it. It's like other things: It takes practice."

The balloon sat in the middle of his bedroom floor, having been jostled from its place beneath Gary's bed. It had lost air. Without asking, Vickie began tapping the balloon with her hands, and Gary thought how easy it was for her to be in the world without having to know certain things that he knew. He knew what that balloon was. She didn't. She tapped it until, finally, it evaded her and fell to the floor. "I feel like stepping on it," Vickie said. "Can I step on it?" Gary nodded his head. Gary said yes. It was not a huge event, but it did seem like a necessary one.

One nagging thing remained: a cardboard box full of William's shrunken laundry. Barbara had given his other things away—shoes, boots, coats—but these things were ruined, and she couldn't give ruined things away, she said. In the mornings, Gary saw the clothes in the hallway, sitting in a pool of sunlight. What these clothes needed was to be thrown away. But neither Barbara nor Gary could do that to them.

Gary decided that he would try to give them away himself. The Salvation Army was downtown, and Vickie offered to drive him there. She was only fifteen, as was Gary, but edging up against the law excited her. She drove as she did other things, with an easy, adult intuition, one hand on the wheel while she tuned the radio into a country station. A man with a sad, dark pit for a voice sang, "Hold me while you love me, baby. Love me while you hold me." Barbara was at the movies with a girlfriend that afternoon and Gary had taken the car keys from the top of her dresser. Outside, yellow sunlight pressed down on the white mountains and the icy roadsides. Vickie drove too fast on the interstate, reaching almost ninety-five in Barbara's apple green Buick. "She goes," Vickie said. "She really goes." She took pleasure in this, while Gary worried. He was afraid of being caught. He was afraid—though he couldn't say why—for the clothes.

Vickie's parking skills were poor. The huge green car slanted at thirty degrees from the curb. They had dented the car in front of them. They were leaving marks behind. "Oh God. Oh God," Gary said.

"Shush up," Vickie said. "Nobody saw us." Indeed, nobody had.

At the counter where people handed clothing in, the homeless loitered in their knit hats and layered sweaters and coats. They drank coffee out of Styrofoam cups and Big Gulps from the 7-Eleven down the road. Homelessness, Gary thought, was a look that smeared itself onto you. He wanted to believe that all these people needed was a good bath. He wanted suffering to be simpler than it was.

"We can't take these," the man at the counter said. He had a carbuncular nose shot through with burst vessels. "People think that we'll take anything they want to give us. That's just not true." Gary sympathized with this man: Receiving charity all day must make you grumpy. But he also remembered the robber—the urgent need of the robber to take. What Gary felt now was a ferocious need to give. Had he had a gun, he would have made this man take his father's clothes. He would have said, Take them or die, motherfucker.

Instead, Vickie and Gary placed the box on a nearby corner and sat at a Wendy's across the street, drinking coffee and smoking and watching the box to see what the world would do to it. The plastic caps of their paper coffee cups said, CAUTION: CONTENTS MAY BE EXTREMELY HOT. Even coffee cups told you to be afraid. On one flap of the box, Vickie had written in ballpoint pen, "These clothes are for you. Please take." Gary thought of those strange words: How odd for a box to pretend to say something like that.

For a long time, nothing happened. People walked around the box. Finally a teenage boy dressed in army fatigues rummaged through it and took a shirt and some pants. He seemed to have friends, who came after him and rummaged, too. The box attracted a circle of young people. Gary felt that some distant desire—not quite his own—had been satisfied now. He felt the world expand a little. Vickie said, "See? Sometimes things just take care of themselves."

They drove away in the green Buick that afternoon, leaving no note on the dented car in front of them. They had done well. They had left behind exactly what they had needed to leave behind. "Ha!" Vickie said, accelerating past a green light, the wheels of the Buick squealing, and the force of the engine pulling Gary back in his seat as the huge car lurched forward.

VISIONS

It was Halloween and I was about to lose my fourth job that fall, this one as the pool man at the YMCA in Salt Lake City, when a little girl, the first one to jump in after the five P.M. cleaning, came out screaming and seeing nothing but white. She wore a blue one-piece suit with cartoon figures of Donald Duck printed all over it. She was a little blond, blue-eyed girl, a darling little girl, I guess you'd say. I'd never been a genius at math and I'd gotten the ratios wrong. I had a drinking problem, too, and, earlier that day, had taken a quick afternoon break at My Ex-Wife's Place, a bar about a block away from the Y on State, where I'd put down a few doubles, and gotten back to the pool feeling pretty good and just in time to do the five P.M. cleaning. The paramedics came and pinned down the girl, who, until then, had been running helter-skelter through the arms of screaming mothers. They stuck a needle in her and, in seconds, she lay there at peace, her eyes opened in this glassy stare while the medics waved their hands in front of her. "How many fingers? How many fingers?"

I kept saying, "Three ... three fingers." But she didn't say anything.

"Goddamn you, Mitchell!" Lutz, my boss, said. He'd

taken me into his office and was throwing one of those round lifesaver doughnuts into the blue tile wall. Throwing and throwing it. A paper mobile of smiling skeletons—Halloween decorations—hung from the ceiling. "It's our asses, you know."

Outside the office, the little girl's mother beat at the glass window—the kind with wire mesh run through it—and screamed, *"Bastard! Bastard!"* with her eyes pushed up to the window, looking at me through the little wires. I said, "Tell her I'm sorry. Will you tell her I'm sorry?"

Lutz said, "You are sorry, Mitchell," though, of course, he'd meant a different kind of sorry.

When I got home, my boys were beating the little white things out of an old beanbag chair, and my wife smelled of fish from the tuna casserole cooking in the oven. I turned the oven light on and looked through the little window at the casserole. It was bubbling on top. I got the dishes out and began setting the table, first the plates and napkins, then the silverware. I hoped doing a few simple tasks would save me.

I'd always thought of blindness as being in the dark. But this little girl saw a light that she couldn't look into. It was a temporary condition, something the chemicals had done to her, though I didn't know that then. I imagined her spending the rest of her life in a universe of scorching light. I imagined how the world would flay her every time she opened her eyes.

My wife said, "The school counselor called about Jordan today. He bit another boy on the face and the boy bled. The counselor says that Jordan is angry about something. The counselor wants to know if everything's all right at home. The counselor asked, 'Is everything all right with you folks at home?'" She was shaking a metal serving spoon at me. She must have thought I'd been drinking, the way she looked at me then. The girl with the Donald Duck suit was still screaming in my head. Then I noticed that I had a bottle of Jack in my hand and I remembered how I'd driven from the pool to the liquor store and then home. I remembered how Jack, not the whiskey but the clerk at the liquor store, whom I'd gotten to know pretty well, said, "Up to no good on Halloween, are ya?" and how I'd hated him for saying something that was truer than he knew. I lifted the bottle up between my wife and me now, just to let her know I wasn't trying to hide anything.

"Something happened," I said.

"You're so talented," she said. "You're so goddamn talented, Mitchell." This was how Jean referred to my drinking—"my talent," she called it. It was one of those words that came from her knowing me a little too well and not liking what she knew about me.

"I blinded a little girl today." I'd had enough to drink by then to be truthful.

She said, "What?"

I explained it to her as best I could and got choked up and started saying things that didn't need to be said. "She was wearing this blue swimming suit with little pictures of Donald Duck on it, you know."

Then my wife said what I was thinking. "That little girl," she said. "That poor little girl."

I looked down at the floor. The yellow linoleum seemed to teeter. I guess I was learning to what degree bad things could happen to me. On the refrigerator door was a picture my younger boy, Powell, had drawn some months ago. It said "DAD" on it. My portrait had a huge lopsided head and a body of squiggly blue lines with a pulpy gob of red crayon in the middle of my chest that was supposed to be my bleeding heart. He knew me. I saw that my little boy knew me.

Jean began throwing things into suitcases—her clothes, some towels, some of the boys' clothes. In between packing things, she said, "You're just one stupid tragedy after the next, Mitchell."

I said, "Jean, honey, look at me." She didn't. "I don't want to hear that you're leaving me again." She had left me before, though only for an afternoon or an evening, and she had never packed an actual suitcase.

"Think of that little girl." She said that twice, first in a voice that was sad for the girl and then in a voice that was furious at me.

"I think of her," I said. "I think of her. I do, Jean."

She gripped Powell's stuffed mule—its name was Hee-haw—by the muzzle and shook it at me in a way that looked painful to my little boy's toy. "This time I'm really leaving you, Mitchell."

I said, "What do you need Heehaw for? Heehaw can stay here."

"I don't need Heehaw," she said. "Your little boy needs him."

"But we're getting better," I said. "Aren't we?" This was how we'd always spoken of my problem. We said it was "ours" and that "we" had to deal with it. I liked this way of speaking about it, because things felt like they were being worked on and getting done with two of us putting out the effort.

But now she said, "We . . . we!" in a tone of voice I didn't like the sound of. She threw the stuffed animal into the suitcase and closed it. "You still have your eyes, Mitchell, and that little girl doesn't."

"What do my eyes have to do with this?" But right after I'd said that, I understood her point. "I'd give her my eyes if I could. Really, Jean. I'd give her my eyes. In a minute."

Jean held the keys to the Ford truck—our only vehicle—fisted up in her hand. Outside the weather was white and colorless and I felt the evening coming on and didn't want to have to be the one to stay, to walk through the quiet rooms afterward, alone with what I'd done that day. I tried to pry the keys from Jean's fist, but she was angrier than I was, and that made her strong. When I finally got the keys, she rode me piggyback down the hall, digging her nails into my neck and kicking my sides with her pink Keds, saying, "You . . . you . . . you!" The boys were watching a World War II film. Cannon fire and the choppy sounds of Japanese screamed through our house. When we got to the living room, they turned away from the set and looked at us. Behind them, a Japanese Zero crashed into the sea and their war movie came to a moment of peace in which nothing but ten or fifteen seconds of endless ocean—water and no land as far as you could see—glowed from the screen, so that the air in the darkening room was a fissured, aquatic blue. Powell started bawling and I wanted to calm him down, because I had decided to believe that all of this was going to blow over in a few minutes and we'd be into that casserole.

"Nothing to worry about, pal," I said.

Jean said, "Turn around and watch TV." They did. She hiked her knees up and pressed them into my ribs, and her nails were still doing a hell of a job on my neck and shoulders. I used the walls of the entryway to try to get her off, but she stayed on until I fell over on the front lawn, where the keys rattled across the brown grass and she scooped

them up, brushed the leaves off her jeans, and went back
in for the suitcases and the boys.

I rolled onto my back and saw the chalky sky through
the black branches of the elm and started to remember the
little girl again and how she hadn't been able to see the
fingers that the EMTs had held up to her and how I had
seen them so clearly—three fingers with wrinkled knuckles
and brief curls of dark hair growing from the wrinkles—
three, exactly three.

Powell walked over to me and I looked at his blue sneakers, then up at him at this strange angle that made him
seem giant, with a large sloping upper body and a head and
red face the size of a man's. He didn't look like my little
boy up there. "Daddy," he said. "You did something wrong,
didn't you?"

"Hey, trooper," I said back to him. His mother hurried
by and swooped him up in her arm. "See you soon, little
guy. Maybe tomorrow," I said.

"No," his mother said. "Not tomorrow."

"He did something wrong, didn't he?" he asked his
mother now.

I heard Jordan say, in a voice that was pretty angry for
a twelve-year-old, "He's drunk. He's just drunk."

"Don't use that tone with me, wise guy," I said, trying to
pick myself up off the ground.

"What did he do wrong?" my little boy asked again.

I was still trying to stand up.

"We're not going to talk about it now," their mother said.
She was tossing my belongings out of the truck cab—a
plastic cup, some Coke cans, bottle tops, and a few empty
packages of Camels. The wind rose and my things skittered
down the street and into the neighbors' yards. By the time

I was on my feet again, my family had already driven down the street and around the corner, on their way to Jean's parents, who lived on the other side of the valley from us.

"All right, folks," I heard the TV say from inside my house. Dusk had come and there was something shabby and unclean about the half-light. All at once, the night seemed to swirl downward like the rush of dirty water down a drain and the windows of the neighboring houses went inward with a clean yellow glow that pulled at you with warmth.

Hal, my next-door neighbor, walked out of his front door wearing a dark, furry costume, carrying his little girl in one arm and what looked like some sort of head in the other.

"Hi ya, Mitchell," he said.

Janice, his wife, walked out behind him, a husky woman dressed in the black garments of a witch. Her face was large and greasy and not very attractive. "Hi ya," she also said. They had probably heard or seen some of what had just happened to me and seemed awkward and reticent.

"On our way to the church Halloween party," Hal said. "Bob for apples, you know."

The little girl in Hal's arms was dressed in a pink body-suit and a hood topped with two small animal ears. I guessed she was some sort of rodent—a rabbit, a mouse. The porch light fell over her face and glowed there like a nimbus, an aura. "I don't like him," she said, obviously meaning me. "His face is dark."

"Shush," her father said. Then to me: "Kids . . . kids." I had no idea what she'd meant, though I felt it—a darkness, some sort of hideous bruise or filth over my face, a mark of what I had become that day, which maybe only the kid could see.

"My husband's an ape this year," Janice said.

He lifted up the head of that animal on his fist. "See?" he said.

"I see," I said, not knowing how to continue a conversation that had started that way and beginning to think that, as bad as my life was, I wouldn't want to be one of them, though that certainly didn't mean I wanted to be me.

I got away from them when the phone rang inside my house. "I'm still at the office," my boss said. His voice was calm. "I just want to warn you that we're going to file negligence charges against you, Mitchell."

"Sure," I said.

"You want to know about the girl?"

"Know about her?"

"How she's doing," he said.

"No," I said.

"Well, she's fine," he said. "We're still going to fire your ass, Mitchell. But they rinsed the stuff out of her eyes and she sees as well as she ever has, all right?"

I said, "Sure . . . sure," though what he had said didn't register with me then and wouldn't register with me until the next morning. Still dressed in my pajamas, I would go out to the garage to dig in the toolbox for a flask of whiskey I remembered hiding once. I pulled out screwdrivers and pliers and a large hammer, but no whiskey, none. Thirsty as hell, I recalled what Lutz had possibly said the night before. I called him up that morning and he said, "Yeah, that's what I said," and I was no longer the man I thought I had become the day before. I was like Scrooge on Christmas, only it was Halloween, and I had gotten to see what I might have become and now had a second chance, though what I really wanted then was another drink, a thing I wouldn't stop wanting until I found out Jean had left me for good and I could visit my kids only if I sobered up, which I finally did.

But that night, I didn't know any of this. I had still blinded a little girl. Outside, trick-or-treaters walked through the grainy light of streetlamps accompanied by adults because the year before a boy of eight had been doused by gasoline and lit up only a mile away from our neighborhood, and that frightened people. Jean had been pretty well prepared with six bags of those bite-sized candy bars and I poured the candy into bowls, fixed myself a tall glass of Jack, and sat down in front of the TV. I had decided to watch it with my eyes closed because I wanted to make myself suffer the darkness that I had put that little girl in. I was confused and drunk and I wanted to feel like a better person somehow, the kind of person who struggles to understand the pain he causes others. I knew that sitting in front of the TV with my eyes closed was not a large enough gesture and would do nothing to save me from what I'd done, but I didn't know what else to do.

I leaned my head back and felt the darkness cover me like a blanket, lush and heavy from all the liquor I had drunk that night. It pressed thickly against my face, as if it were shaping me and my face was taking on that strange mute aspect of the blind, who never see themselves. I forgot my eyes and I thought, Yes, yes, now you're blind, Mitchell. Now you'll never see again. I heard a storm blowing from inside the TV and the sounds of waves and a man's voice, shredded like a rope about to break, calling another man's name. "Charlie! Charlie!" it called.

I lost courage then and opened my eyes. But a commercial had come on and the doorbell was ringing.

———

I spent the rest of that night answering the door to loud shouts of "Trick or treat!" and greeting bunches of little monsters—vampires, ghouls, hunchbacks, zombies—on my doorstep. At first I felt safe from them. I convinced myself that so long as I couldn't see who they really were behind their costumes, they couldn't see me, either. But I was clumsy with the handfuls of Three Musketeers and Milky Ways, now and then missing the pillowcases and plastic pumpkins that the kids carried their candy in. "You're drunk," a man said. His little boy had a large trick eyeball molded into the center of his forehead and swung a toy ax in my direction. "You're drunk . . . you're drunk," the boy said, mimicking his father and aiming his third eye at me.

After I closed the door, I went to the living room window and watched that man stop on the corner of my lawn, where, in the light of the streetlamp, he grabbed his kid's candy sack, dug out the candy I had just given them, and threw it out on my lawn. The kid kept screaming, "My candy! My candy! My candy!"

I poured myself another glass of Jack and tried to maintain my best holiday mood, though, to tell the truth, I was tired of the monsters coming to my door. The kids seemed too excited about dressing in their evil costumes and acting out their cruel urges. Of course, it was just a game to them, and there was—thank God—the occasional little girl who had chosen to be something—a princess, an angel, a goddess—prettier and happier than she could have been in real life. I favored these girls, giving the Tinker Bells and Snow Whites and Cinderellas and Princess Leias larger handfuls of candy bars and saying about their brothers and little boyfriends, "I don't see why they should get good stuff for being ugly, do you?" even though that kind of comment may not have been in the best spirit of Halloween.

FIRST SEX

On his eighteenth birthday, Henry Black assumed that, despite the passage of one more year and despite his very recent and very first girlfriend, Carol Green, he would remain the same Henry Black as before: a gifted high school mathematician headed from Madline, Idaho, to MIT in the fall, an elder in the Mormon Church, one of only three Eagle Scouts ever to hail from Madline, a decent boy who, until that afternoon as he tutored Carol Green in math, felt he needed only the American ethic to get by in life—hard work, the God of his church, and love—though not necessarily the kind of love that Carol Green expressed when, in one seamless gesture, she knelt on the carpeted floor of her bedroom, undid Henry's pants, and gave him his first ever oral sex immediately after he had shown her how to solve for x and y in a quadratic equation. Henry Black had known of Carol Green at Skygate High ever since they were freshmen, had seen her smoking her Kool cigarettes out in the parking lot behind the school, had even—to his terror—thought he could just make out the faint seam of her vagina through the very tight jeans that she always wore. But they had not met until two weeks ago, when he finally approached her—she sat three desks over from him in Mr.

Bunion's college algebra class, which, Henry knew, she was failing terribly—and offered to tutor her every day after school, not least because she resembled, despite the tight, tight denim she wore, his favorite movie heroine ever, Scarlett O'Hara, whom, since he was eight, he and his mother and older sisters had traveled once a year all the way to the Avalon theater in Salt Lake City, 120 miles over the Utah border, to see once more declare beneath a clod of upheld dirt after an hour and a half of war and love that she would never, never go hungry again, a scene that made Henry weep every time. Carol was the very likeness of her, with her silky brunette waves, her single mole, as fine and black as chocolate, on her left cheek, not to mention the Technicolor purple of her lips, which she got from always chewing on a wad of grape bubble gum. The first time she kissed him—just last week—with her deep-fuchsia tongue, she pulled away and took him in with her green eyes and said, "I've never liked a smart guy before. You're my first one." Though he hadn't known how much she liked him until this afternoon when she distinguished herself forever from Scarlett O'Hara and pressed him up against her bedroom wall with one hand and helped herself to his privates with her other. He had never witnessed such ease, such simple, straightforward delving into the forbidden as he did then, looking down at what Carol Green was doing for him.

"You look scared," she said now. "Don't you like it?"

"Yes," he said. He was scared and he did like it, even if he had to force himself not to think of the good boy that he was supposed to be, the honor-role student who had known only the kind of love his mother, Crystal, had given him as a little boy when she put him to bed, asked Jesus in her prayers to forgive them, sinners both, and kissed him, once on each cheek and a third time on the forehead, kisses

that had hardly prepared him for the sort of kiss he was
receiving now or for the thing that Carol Green, pausing
from her work down below, said to him then.

"Do you want me to take off my shirt so that you can
see me?"

He didn't get around to answering her question before
she pulled her T-shirt—which said, UNCLE TED'S OIL
SHOP, TEN MINUTE FULL SERVICE OIL CHANGE, $19.95 on
it—all the way off, along with her bra.

"There," she said, taking one of his hands from his side
and cupping it just so over the nipple part of her breast.
"You can touch me, silly."

This was a basic truth, about which he was only now
learning. He could touch her, in fact was now touching and
feeling with his right hand—the one he'd just been solving
for x and y with—the heat of real-in-the-flesh breast. At
the same time, he had to listen to her father—the Uncle
Ted of the only oil and lube service in Madline—bang
around the kitchen. *Slam* went a drawer. *Clop, clop* went
Ted's heavy feet. *Slam* went another drawer, after which
he—the very man who had lubed and serviced for years
the Blacks' Suburban and their Chevy Malibu and Henry's
own 1972 GMC Blazer—hurdled his voice, black as cast
iron, right at her locked bedroom door. "What you two
doing in there?" he said.

Carol took her mouth from Henry's penis. "Algebra!" she
shouted back.

Henry was trembling, so afraid that he looked away from
the sin they were committing and over at the algebra book,
broken open to the page where Henry had just solved three
quadratic equations for Carol, each computation aligned in
neat columns and numbered so that Carol could learn how
it was done, which she hadn't learned. She had instead

looked out her bedroom window, where, on that February afternoon, a slate-colored snowstorm slanted down over the fields of mud and cow shit as far as you could see, then looked back at Henry with her eyes as green as the first day of summer and said, "How come equations are so easy for you?"

"It just comes natural."

"Nature put those numbers in you?"

"I guess," Henry had answered, which was true. He really had surmised that these numbers, these computations and equations, were his nature, and had not guessed otherwise until she said next, "I want to give you your birthday present now, Henry Black," enunciating his last name—Black—as if it were a piece of fudge cake she had just closed up in her mouth, consumed, and melted down. He had never heard his name cuddled so at the bottom of a wet, female voice. Then she stood him up and performed the act that was about to change his ideas about everything.

"Stop being so afraid," she said now, kissing and nibbling at the blade of his hipbone and doing something with her hand—a certain turn, touch motion—that he knew he'd want again and again. "Daddy's not going to do anything."

"My mother expects me home soon," Henry said, hearing the fear in his own voice. He didn't know how they'd gotten into this conversation about their parents, but he wanted to leave it—he wanted to leave it fast.

"We're almost there," she said, going back to giving him his birthday present, while Henry fought off the thought of what his mother was doing for him just then a half mile down the road in her kitchen, where her hands would be covered in the buttery yellow batter of what would soon become his very favorite cake, the one he had always gotten on his birthday, what was called a Lady Baltimore cake,

three layers covered in vanilla frosting and sprinkled in co-
conut shavings, the whole thing as white and formidable as
a Victorian petticoat, a towering dessert, though one that he
quickly forgot now as Carol said again, "We're almost
there!" And then they were there. In the next instant, between her mouth and himself, Henry felt a whole mountain
range spring up, over which he fell backward into some
kind of flowery meadow of pleasure.

"You love me, don't you?" Carol said. When he opened
his eyes again, Carol was wiping the corners of her mouth
with her bundled-up T-shirt.

"Uh-huh," Henry said. And he *did* love her. He felt it
inside him, a pink zero-gravity sensation that fled upward
from his groin to his head. That was love, and he continued
to experience it until she came up and kissed him on the
mouth and Henry Black tasted himself, a bland, unclean,
biological taste that made him feel sad and dirty, human
and ugly, that made him wish he were a cleaner, better boy,
and that made him even want to flee Carol Green, who had
put her bra and a fresh T-shirt on, as well as a wintergreen
Cert in her mouth so that her daddy couldn't smell it. "Sex
has a smell," she said in a hushed voice.

She knew too much about all the wrong things. But it
was true. Sex did have a smell, and Henry Black smelled
it—perspiration and semen, along with a close, moist odor
of groin and skin—somewhere in the room and it worried
him and made him still sadder.

"What's wrong, Henry?" Carol asked. "Aren't you happy
to turn eighteen?"

She brushed a hand through his hair, a gentle gesture
that relieved him so much from the shock of first sex that
he spoke honestly now. "I feel sort of dirty," he said, "and
sad, too." He let himself fall backward over Carol's bed,

spent, his hands so numb and lifeless that he couldn't seem to summon the energy to pull his pants up, and instead sat there looking at the terrible whiteness of his briefs scrunched down around his knees, so that all he could do was try once again not to think of his mother, who had bought these very briefs at the Madline Woolworth's and bleached them once a week, folded them, and put them in his top drawer, which smelled of flowers and detergent every time he opened it. No, he was not going to think about her now. He was not going to think about the absolute goodness of clean laundry, folded and shut away in his drawer.

"You think too much, Henry," Carol said now, lying down on the bed with him. "Besides, you liked it. Your eyes got all fishy and wide. I know that look." She cuddled up beside him and did the one thing that would stay with him even more than the memory of his first oral sex, the one thing he would remember not just for the rest of his eighteenth birthday but for the days and weeks and years after it. She pulled his pants up and—to his astonishment—gently and thoughtfully arranged his penis beneath the tight hug of his underwear, laying it down along the line of his navel as if she had known all along exactly how it best liked to lie, before lifting her hand, like a strange flower, to her nose and smelling it. "That's you," she said, smiling at him. "Here." She put her hand in his face now. What else could he do? He didn't want to. In fact, it was the last thing Henry Black wanted to do on the first day of his nineteenth year, the year in which he would become legally and officially available to die for his country, a fact that somehow bothered him less than what Carol Green was now holding before him. But he was tired and vulnerable, so he did it. So he smelled her hand. So he felt his innocence drain from him. So all the love his mother had given him fell finally and securely into question. Not that it was false. But it and her clean laundry and her many years of Lady Baltimore cakes, as well as Margaret Mitchell's burning fields of love and war, were all just a dream compared to the very real stink of his crotch on Carol Green's palm, which claimed him now. "That's you," she said again, smiling, as if this fact were a beautiful thing. And maybe it was. He was trying not to cry, and he succeeded, thank God, though he would have certainly failed had she not just then put her hand down and wiped it clean on her bedsheets. For on this afternoon of his eighteenth birthday, Henry Black was not the Eagle Scout, not the good son, not the mathematician on his way from Madline to MIT, not the potential soldier for his country; he was, instead, the smell of his penis on Carol Green's palm. That's who he was. And maybe for one afternoon on a very gray day in Madline, Idaho, that wasn't such a bad thing to be. Maybe it was even the inevitable and human thing to be, which was a thought Henry would have liked to lie on his back with and look at the ceiling for an hour or so while it weighed in him. But instead, Carol said, "Happy birthday, Henry," for no apparent reason—she was still a mystery to him—before adding one last comment that he had not expected and that left him again staring into the darkness of the unknown. "You're going to have to do me next time." Then, proving that she could read his frightened mind or that he simply could not hide it, she said, "Don't worry. I'll show you how. It's nice."

But he did worry, and worried even more when Carol's father knocked—in fact, it seemed more like a pounding— just as Henry was thinking how good it was to have between him and Carol and every adult he had ever known a locked door. "Dinner," her father said. "Open up," which was exactly what Henry did not want her to do. He needed one more minute—one more, please—to think of how he was going to face the oil and lube man, the father of the daughter who had just given him what she had given him, not to mention his own family, his father and four sisters, his mother and her towering dessert, above which he would soon sit and hide the new naked spot that Carol had shown him at the back of his soul as the candles that he would blow out smoldered, as a wish for his future formed in him, as his mother would look up at him and say, "Happy birthday, Henry dear," without ever guessing who or what Henry had become that day. One more minute, please. But Carol Green did not even give him that. Beautiful and unafraid, she leapt from the bed and opened the door.

Liars

On the day before Christmas, my father called out of the blue, as was his habit, and begged my mother to let me ski with him that day. This was years ago, when I was fourteen. My father liked to see me on his own terms and on his own time, which was just one of the things my mother hated him for. The thing she most hated him for was his having left her when I was eighteen months and she was a first-time mother of twenty-two, newly arrived in Salt Lake City and lonely and living in a way she had not foreseen for herself.

She had been working with cookie dough when he called, and bits of moist flour clung to the receiver as she told him definitely not. That night, we were having relatives over, some of whom had come from as far as two states away and were staying in the Red Roof Inn downtown. I knew, by the look on her face, that he was making promises to her—crossing his heart and pledging his honor. I heard my father's voice say, "I'll have the boy home by six. No excuses."

"Look, Bill," she said, "we're having dinner at six and then we're going to services. He's staying at home."

My mother looked at me from the side of her eyes. She

knew I was listening. I had no other reason to sit at the kitchen table and stare out the window at the falling snow. It had been coming down in heavy sideways sheets all morning and it was hard to see anything beyond it. "You want to go, Malcolm?" she asked. The tone of her voice made it pretty clear that she hoped I would say no. Her mouth was set hard and she had a streak of white flour across her chin where she'd accidentally touched herself.

"I don't know," I said. "Maybe."

"Maybe," she said back at me. "What does *maybe* mean?"

I heard my father say something, to which my mother quickly said, "You stay out of this."

"Well," she said, "you want to go or not?"

I said, "You don't want me to go, do you?"

My father tried to say something again, but she held the phone away from her and gagged the receiver with her fist. "It's your decision, Malcolm. He says he'll have you back by six." We both knew that my father had a hard time keeping promises. "Let's say this," she said. "We know we can't trust him, right? So let's make you responsible for getting home by six. Can you do that for us?"

"Okay," I said. "I'll go."

"By six," she told me again. "Let's not let him ruin our Christmas."

Then she said too loudly into the receiver, "He's going."

After she'd hung up, she looked at me, her folded arms white with flour. "Promise me one thing, Malcolm," she said. I shook my head. "Don't let them talk about me and don't let them talk down about us going to church." "Them" was my father and his latest girlfriend, Beaty.

I told her I wouldn't, but she didn't seem to believe me. "Stick up for us," she said. "Don't let him be a bully." Then, seeing right through me, she said, "I wouldn't let myself get so excited about this afternoon's ski trip. He might not even show up. You know how he is."

But he did show up. About an hour after he called, he and Beaty—her real name was Beatrice—came to pick me up in his truck. There was just enough room in the cab for me to squeeze in between them. My father drank coffee from his Duck's Unlimited travel mug and wore a pair of aviator glasses with yellow lenses and smelled like the Dutch tobacco that he and Beaty rolled their own cigarettes with. He had some tools—screwdrivers and pliers—a role of black electrician's tape, and a buck knife in a leather scabbard out on the dash. One of those pine tree air fresheners dangled from the rearview mirror, though it was old and didn't smell like anything. I accidentally stepped on Beaty, who was in her socks, when I climbed in. "Watch it, Malcolm!" she said. Beaty had her thick ski clothes on. Her face was done up and she smelled of a slightly harsh perfume—acidic flowers—and was, I remember, a more attractive woman than my mother, tall and thin, with fine features and a tan complexion, though I didn't much like her looks. I thought she was arrogant, too aware of her appearance, though I'm not sure now that I had any real reason to feel that way.

My mother came to the window of the truck, her breath smoking in the air, and my father looked at her, raised his right hand, and said, "Scout's honor, Pam. We'll have him home, ready to go, by six." He put his other arm around me as if to show that he had the goods in hand. My mother didn't look in Beaty's direction until Beaty spoke to her.

"Thanks for letting us have him for the afternoon," she said.

When we pulled out of the driveway, Beaty sighed. "It's hard to be so polite all the time."

"Let's not start with that," my father said.

"It's Christmas," she said. "I don't see why Pam thinks that she's the only—"

"Lay off it, Beaty," my father said.

"Okay already," she said. She was cheerful now, a trait that my father loved in people. He loved happy people. "All right, Malcolm, look at me and smile."

"Come on," I said. She was a dental hygienist and part of her act with me was to examine my teeth.

"Smile," she said. "Crack a big old sunrise in my direction." I finally did this and she said, "Stellar, kiddo. Both you and your father have nice teeth." She touched my face and I pulled away from her a little.

"So what do you think of the new ski suit that your father bought me?" She stretched herself out in the crowded cab and smiled to show that she was an eager model. "Well," she said, "what do you think?"

"I like it," I said, lying. It was a bright yellow bodysuit that zipped up the front and had probably cost my father more than a few bucks.

"It's good to be with you, Malcolm," she said. "You know that I enjoy your company, don't you?"

"Sure," I said.

She pulled me into a hug that I didn't quite warm or soften to. "Too old for all this lovey stuff, aren't you?" I smiled at her without saying anything.

We stopped for gas at the mouth of Big Cottonwood Canyon and my father got out and talked to the old man who ran the place while Beaty and I waited in the truck. The old man's parka was hunter's orange and so stuffed with down that his wrinkled body seemed to recede into its fluorescent depths. He smoked a cigarette, which didn't seem like a smart thing to do around gas pumps, and he was almost shouting at my father. I could just make out his words from inside the cab. "It's pretty damn tricky up there today." My father just laughed, as if that were some sort of joke.

I looked at my watch; we had just over five hours, and I wasn't sure how we would get up and down in that amount of time with the snow still falling and the canyon roads covered. "Stop that," Beaty said. "We have plenty of time. You're going to ruin our fun if you worry all day."

I said, "I'm not worried." The heater was blasting warm air, but the cab was chilly and the windows were covered in a wet skin of moisture, through which we could still see my father walking with the old man across the parking lot and gesturing up at the mountain. He stood a full head taller than the old man and had broad shoulders and an easy gait.

"I know your mother hates him," Beaty said. "But I just hope you understand what a beautiful and generous man your father is. I hope you appreciate him."

"I know that," I said.

"He's kind of a loner," she said. "He does things his own way. I like that about him." Even though he had walked into the station and out of our view, Beaty still stared in his direction, and so did I.

"He hurts people," I said, wishing right away that I hadn't said that.

"You're not in a very good mood today," she said. She started tapping her painted nails against the dash. "Is that what your mother tells you about him?"

"No," I said. "Nobody needs to tell me that." But my mother had said this more than once, and, as far as I could see, it was true. He had hurt a lot of women after my mother, women who, in my opinion, were better than Beaty. His relationships lasted for maybe six months. Beaty had been with him for eight, so I figured she was about to get hers.

She tilted the rearview mirror in her direction, wiped the condensation away with her hand, and began to apply lipstick, stretching her lips into an O shape, then clamping them down. When she spoke to me now, her teeth seemed larger, more vividly white and distinct behind her bright red lips. "I've got a bulletin for you, kiddo. Ready for this one?" I looked away toward the whirling orange hood light of a snowplow dragging its noisy blade up the canyon road. "Malcolm," she said in a commanding tone that meant I had to look at her again. My father had just exited the station and was walking toward the truck, waving in our direction. I looked back at Beaty. "Thank you," she said. "Your father and I are talking about settling down. You know—tying the knot. I just thought you should know that. I thought you should have some time to think about it. Maybe you could start liking me. What do you think?"

I looked down at my watch again. "Hey," she said, "stop that."

My father opened the door and sat down, a flurry of snow falling on his side of the seat. His hair and beard were white and crystallized from the cold and he flashed us a smile. "How the troops doing?"

"Malcolm keeps looking at his watch. He's going to be a worrywart," she said.

"No I'm not," I said.

"We have all the time in the world," he said. "When I was your age, I wasn't half so excited about getting to church on time."

I felt my stomach tighten and knew that I should defend myself and my mother then. I also knew that if I chose not to, I would probably lose the right to do it later that day. But the words didn't come, so I covered my watch with the sleeve of my parka and said nothing.

At the ski resort, we parked in an empty, snow-covered lot and got out and sat on the tailgate to put our boots on. We were in a fog. The visibility was about twenty feet and I could barely make out the red glow of somebody else's tailgate on the other side of the lot. "We drove into a cloud or something," Beaty said. "How are we supposed to ski when we can't see?" The snowfall was still thick and cottony, but the wind had died and it was quiet. I could hear car doors slam now and somebody's voice say, "This is so weird," and the hum of ski lifts somewhere above us.

But twenty minutes later, after we had taken three lifts up to the top of the mountain, we rose out of the haze a little and could see the hard gray sky and the narrow icy chain of the Wasatch Range breaking out of the crud lower down. The slopes were windblown and trackless with deep snow and the whiteness of the mountain hurt to look at. The red color of my father's parka gave me focus and balance, and I tried to keep it in sight as we skied. But he was a powerful skier and stayed ahead of us, rarely glancing back. Beaty was the more elegant skier, her shoulders always to the hill as she glided through turns and left a single track in her wake. I skied aggressively, even if that meant sloppy form, determined to stay a good stretch in front of Beaty's pretty, self-conscious skiing and as close to my father as I could. For a time, I trailed him, coming near enough to hear the swish and click of his poles and skies, but eventually I needed to rest and he didn't. He kept pumping down the mountain, sailing around a farther and farther bend, until I saw only the red of his parka in the haze, then not even that much. By the time Beaty and I met him at the bottom of the lift, he had rolled and smoked through half a cigarette. "It doesn't get any better than this," he said.

"How about skiing with us next run?" Beaty said. "We're here, too."

He stood up straight and gave her a military salute, and I laughed at this joke, but Beaty didn't. She was forceful and not at all afraid of him, and I could tell he liked her for that.

We took three more runs in fair-enough weather and in snow that my father kept insisting was as near perfect as snow ever got. The crowds were thin that day—the storm down in the valley had kept them away—and the mountain felt deserted, quiet, and a little lonely to me. I let Beaty and my father ride on the lifts together and sat in the chair behind them, listening to their talk and laughter. They laughed a lot, and I looked at my watch and thought of my mother setting the table—the green tablecloth and red candles and the centerpiece of pinecones—while some of the relatives from Kalispell and Helena arrived a few hours early.

But I tried to keep my mind off that and stay focused on the skiing, which got a lot more difficult later that afternoon when the snow fell in flurries so white and thick and spidery that we could barely see the tips of our skis. None of this bothered my father. "We like this," he said happily as we stood on the cat track at the top of the lift and looked over the edge into the white blur of the slope below.

"We do?" Beaty said. She was wrapping herself up in a thick wool scarf.

"I do," I said.

"Would you slow down this time, Bill? I'd feel better if you kept an eye out for us."

He had taken the last three runs with his usual speed and power and didn't seem about to slow down now. "Sure," he said.

"I'm fine," I said. "You don't need to keep an eye out for me."

"You two just want to be heroes," Beaty said. "I'm cold and I want somebody to ski with me. I don't want heroes."

"You got me," my father said.

For a while, he skied off to the side, from where he tried to coach me out of my wide, sloppy turns. "You're too sideways, kid," he shouted. "Point your skis downhill and go."

"I can't see the ground in this crud," I said.

"It's still there," he said. "Now point yourself downhill and ski."

But I wasn't skiing so hot. I had begun to feel the cold in my fingers and toes. My legs were sore and rubbery. He kept telling me I was skiing shy and to put some speed, some guts, into it, and I tried, but tumbled forward and lost my ski. Beaty came to a stop above me and laughed. "He's trying too hard," she said. "Why don't you just let him ski his way, Bill?"

We were down lower on the mountain now and the wind had calmed. The snowfall was weightless, soft as ash. My father was waiting below Beaty and me, half in the haze, so that we could just see his red outline. "Like this, kid!" he shouted. I watched him as he pointed his skis downhill and lunged into the burned-out air and was gone.

It was just Beaty and me then. She lay down in the snow above me while I dug for my ski, frustrated and hating my father for doing the same as he always did, for saying one thing and doing another. But it wasn't the first time I had hated him, and it never lasted long.

"He's predictable, isn't he?" Beaty said.

"You don't have to wait for me," I said with a little too much meanness. "You can go if you want."

She laughed at me then. "You're angry," she said. "You're angry at him." I had found my ski and was now struggling to get my boot into the binding.

"Has your father always been like this?" she asked.

"Like what?"

"Never mind. I don't want to be inappropriate." My ski snapped into place. "You know, a player. Has he always been a player?"

"What's a player?"

"You like to act dumb, don't you?" I didn't say anything. But it was true. I knew, or thought I knew, what she meant and didn't want to let on because her ideas seemed dangerous for reasons that I didn't understand so well. "A player is someone who tricks you into wanting them more than they deserve to be wanted. That's what your father's done to us."

I was beginning to wish she wasn't saying these things. "He hasn't tricked me," I said. "And I'm not the one who wants him so much."

"Boys want their fathers," she said, "especially when their fathers ski down the mountain without looking back. That's his trick."

I showed her that my ski was on. "We can go now."

"First," she said, "I've got a little confession to make." Above us, a skier in a bright blue bodysuit appeared out of the haze, lunged through the deep snow to our right, leaving a wake of powder and screaming crazily just before he disappeared into the cottony air again. "Hotdogger," Beaty said. Then she looked at me and smiled. "Maybe your father only hurts some people."

"What's your confession?" I asked.

Beaty laughed. "Well," she said, "I was doing a little dreaming earlier today when I told you about your father and me tying the knot. We're not going to marry, Malcolm."

"That's not dreaming," I said. "That's lying."

"Okay," she said. She looked away then and I heard something like shame in her voice, which caught me off guard because I had seen a lot of things in adults—anger and hate and envy and even disgust—but I had not seen shame. I had not seen an adult look away from me the way Beaty had just done. "I lied. I wanted to try it out. But now I'm telling the truth. I thought I'd better tell you before you mentioned it to him. You won't mention it to him, will you?"

"I don't like to be lied to," I said. She didn't say anything, and we sat there for some time with the snow coming down and the white silence of the mountain all around us. I knew then that Beaty must be losing him, and I felt relieved. But I also felt—and this surprised me—bad for her. I felt bad that she had lied, that she had wanted him enough to shame herself in front of me. I had seen other women want my father, too. And I knew that once my mother had wanted him, needed him, and could not have him, which was why she waited for me at home right now, angry and alone. Finally I knew what Beaty did not know or maybe just did not want to know. He did hurt people.

"Sure," I said. "I mean, I won't mention it to him." Then I said, "Why are you always asking me about him?" I wasn't angry. I just wanted to know.

"I thought you might help me know him a little better. That's all."

"No," I said. "I can't help you. I don't know much about him. I mean, I don't understand him. Not like that."

"Of course you don't," she said.

"I'm sorry," I said.

Then she looked at me again and said something that I would remember her saying a long time after Beaty stopped seeing my father. "Silly, kid. You don't have to be sorry for him."

We found my father on the porch of the main lodge, smoking and drinking an Irish coffee in the snowfall, his booted feet crossed and his legs stretched out in front of him. He blew a mouthful of smoke into the air. "Is everyone all right?"

"Thanks for skiing with us for once," Beaty said. She was trying to hide her anger behind a little humor, but it wasn't working. "Would you at least like to say you're sorry, Bill?"

"I'm sorry," he said. "I thought you two were—"

"Of course you did," she said, stepping out of her skis. She sat down across from him at the table, lighted a cigarette, and gave him a very unkind look.

When I began to take my skis off, he said, "Hold on, kid. We've got one more run." Then he turned to Beaty and said, "Hey, I am sorry."

"Tell me more," she said.

He spoke to her in a very soft voice now. "We're going out to dinner tonight, aren't we? Aren't I taking you out? Aren't we going to have a Christmas party, just the two of us?"

"Sure," she said, "and that makes everything okay?"

"Yes," he said. "I think it does." She started to laugh then, and so did he. I guessed they had some sort of personal joke between them.

"Your father's full of shit, Malcolm," Beaty said then, still laughing, still thinking it was all a joke.

But my father did not laugh with her now. He put his drink down and uncrossed his legs. His face had gone hard and he looked at her with a seriousness and coldness that shocked me. "Don't talk about me like that in front of my son, Beaty."

Beaty stopped laughing and looked down at her hands. She had taken her gloves off and I could see that her fingers were trembling a little. A waiter in an orange ski suit began to approach us, then thought better of it and turned away. "It's okay," I said. "I don't mind."

"But I do," my father said. "I mind plenty."

"It was just a joke," Beaty said.

Then my father turned to me and, as if Beaty weren't there at all, said, "One more run, kid?"

I looked at my watch. "It'll be close," I said. In fact, we had more than enough time. But for some reason, I did not want to leave things as they now stood. I wanted my father to say at least one kind word to Beaty, though he was not even looking in her direction now.

"We'll make it a quick one," he said, already getting into his skis and going on about how perfect the snow was, how no other snow on earth was this perfect, how this snow was, as far as he was concerned, a goddamn Christmas miracle.

"I'll wait for you down here," Beaty said.

But my father was already sidestepping for the lift. I wanted to say something to her. "It really didn't bother me," I said.

But that didn't do much. She tried to smile a little. "It's

not a big deal," she said. "Get on now. He's leaving you behind."

And because I didn't want to be left behind, I hurried off in his direction.

From the lift, we could see the weather begin to clear and the pillowy haze thin and curl back and uncover the mountain. Here and there, gnat-size skiers struggled to make their descent. My father took a mini-bottle out of his coat, then uncapped it, took a sip, and passed it to me. "A swig, kiddo."

"If Mom smells that on my breath," I said, "this might be the last time we ski together."

"Who says she's going to smell it?"

"Who says she's not?" I said, because he never seemed to think of that possibility. He always just did a thing and maybe thought about it later.

He put the bottle away. "You're looking better on skis. But you're still afraid of the mountain."

"I'm not afraid of the mountain," I said. "It's just hard to ski in cruddy weather."

"You're sounding like Beaty."

"I'm not Beaty," I said. Then I surprised myself and said, "You don't love Beaty, do you?"

He laughed out loud. "Now you really do sound like Beaty." I saw that he wasn't going to give me an answer and I felt the awkward power of having silenced my father. He put his arm around me and pulled me into him until I smelled the coffee and liquor on his breath. "You're a better person than I am, Malcolm."

"Why do you always do the same thing with women?" I said.

He sat back on his side of the chair then and started

rolling another cigarette. "I think I feel a little heavy weather coming from you, Malcolm."

"It's not heavy weather," I said. "I'd just like to know."

He laughed again, though it was a tired and empty-sounding laughter. "I'd like to know, too," he said. Then he lit his cigarette and smiled at me as if trying to show me that he could still smile. "What am I supposed to say? I'm not proud of myself. I get tired of people. I just do." Then he paused. "There are some things a person can't help."

"You got tired of my mother?" I asked.

"That's ancient history, isn't it, Malcolm?"

"I guess," I said.

"Good," he said, as if we had solved something. "It's my problem and I've always had to live with it, even though I don't like living with it. You understand?"

"Sure," I said, though I didn't understand. For a minute, we sat without talking and just looked up the mountain as the clouds continued to clear and expose the unbroken white of the slopes. We could make out the tiny lift house in the distance now, its Plexiglas front shimmering in a brightness that hurt to look at. As we approached the top, the wind picked up to a dull roar, and I wanted to tell him something. I wanted to tell my father that Beaty was right about him, that he was full of shit, and I shouted it out then as we were putting our skis up and getting ready to dismount. But he hadn't heard me, or chose not to hear me. He just gave me one of his crazy smiles, the wind blowing back the crown of hair that spilled out of his hat. "Let's ski, goddamn it!" he shouted. And then we were doing just that.

My father traversed the eastern slope, a white dust rising behind him, and I followed, keeping my eyes on his red parka, until he stopped above a steep shoot about twenty feet across, unskied, and bordered on both sides by thick forest. Where the sun hit the snow, the white sparkled like a fine dust of diamonds, and I had to look away from that glare. "You first, kid," he said. "Point your skies downhill and go. Can you do that?"

I was tired of that question and leaned forward, kicked my skis over the edge, and felt the hill take me, felt myself slipping, then finding the ground, standing upright, making one and then another turn until I picked up speed.

"Now we're in business," my father said. I heard his poles clicking behind me and then saw him next to me, rising out of his turns. The rhythm I had then was something new, and it seemed strange and uncertain to me, but I kept it. I held my skis out in front and felt a forward momentum and power that must have been natural to him. We were skiing together now as we came out of the shoot and over the top of a treeless bowl, from where we could make out the entire northern slope, white and unmarred, as it swept down to the tiny lift houses below and the flat, plowed parking lots where the few parked cars were as small as toys.

But my legs had already begun to fatigue. "Stay with me, kid," he said. He screamed cheerfully, and so did I, despite the fact that I was done feeling cheerful that day. Breathing hard, struggling against the strange, elongated weight of my skis, I looked over at him and saw that his shoulders were square to the hill, that his arms were tacking rhythmically at his sides, that he had already begun to break away from me. I turned wide and bumped into him. "Watch it," he said, quickly regaining balance and speed. I turned wide again and hit him harder. "Christ!" he shouted. Our shoul-

ders made a dull thud; our skis clattered like sticks. Before
he could recover a second time, I hooked my arm around
his neck and took him down with me.

When I stood up, I saw him laid out in the snow above
me, his hands pinned beneath him and his aviator glasses
and red hat resting on the ground at his shoulders. His chin
was bloodied and his mouth was a red hole, from which
the steam of his breath came heavily. He must have seen it
in my face. "Am I hurt?" He spit, then looked down at the
flecks of red in the snow.

"Just your chin," I said.

"Is my lip still there? I can't feel it." He found his hands
and touched it.

"Don't touch it," I said.

One of his poles was lost and we began digging for it.
But his chin bled into the snow where we dug. "Christ," he
said. "I'm bleeding all over. What does it look like?"

"It's not bad."

"What happened? What the hell did you do back there?"

I didn't answer him.

We left his pole on the mountain and I let him lean on
me as we skied down. But he was shaken and fell twice
more before we reached the lift house, where they gave him
a handful of gauze to hold to the cut and sent us down the
mountain on the ski lift. Despite the cold, his lip bled pretty
good, and the blood got into his turtleneck and made him
look messier and more injured than he was.

"So," he asked me again, "what the hell did you do back
there?" His eyes were glazed and, for the first time that
day, he looked weak, physically drained.

"I just turned wide," I said. "I'm sorry."

"Why would you do something like that, Malcolm?" he asked. He had lifted the gauze to his eyes and was studying the blood that had frozen into the white cotton.

"Do what?" I said.

"You pushed me over, kid."

"No I didn't," I said. It felt terrible to lie to him. "I fell. It was an accident."

"I felt your hands, Malcolm. I felt you grab me. That's not an accidental thing to do. Was it a joke? Was that it?"

I looked at my watch without seeing the time. I didn't need to see it. "Now we're really going to be late," I said.

The doctor at the main lodge was a huge bronze-complected man with green eyes and a blond beard and mustache. A small Christmas tree decorated with white strips of gauze, cotton balls, bandages, and a bit of tinsel sat on the table next to the entrance. Beaty and I sat in orange plastic chairs at the edge of the room while the doctor shined a penlight into my father's pupils, then studied the cut. Both my father and I still had our ski boots on, and the room smelled of medicine and damp wool.

"Looks like you took a ski in the face," the doctor said. "What happened?"

"My boy ran me over," my father said. He sounded more startled than angry now. "He ran right over me."

Beaty started to laugh a little, but I didn't say anything, and the doctor must have sensed something, because he winked at me and said, "That's ten points for the boy."

Beaty laughed some more and looked over at me. "He feels terrible about it. Poor kid."

My father grimaced as the doctor applied a medicated swab to his chin. "It's going to leave a pretty little scar," the doctor said. Then he walked my father into the back room, where he was going to stitch the cut up, and Beaty and I were left alone.

Beaty had gotten out of her yellow ski suit and looked good in her jeans and street shoes and her white turtleneck. She smiled at me and said, "What you looking at, Malcolm?" I looked away from her and she said, "Aren't you the shy one?"

"I'm sorry," I said.

"For what?"

"I don't know," I said.

"He'll survive," she said. "You don't have to worry about him."

"He's not hurt badly," I said.

"Oh," she said, "he's hurt badly enough. He'll feel sorry for himself tonight and want all the sympathy he can get." Then she thought of something else. "Your father and I are going out to dinner tonight," she said. "He's taking us to the Hotel Utah, to that restaurant on the forty-fifth floor. He reserved a window table for us. We'll have a view of the city lights." I thought that was a sad thing to do on Christmas Eve, but she seemed happy about it. "I like views. I like city lights. Your father is better than you think. He knows how to do nice things for women." She smiled, and I understood that she had thought of something then that she couldn't tell me.

"I've got an idea for you," she said. "I think you and I are in the same position, Malcolm." I didn't say anything to her, but I noticed that her hand was in my hair, stroking me, and had been there for some time without me thinking about it, and I sat there now, feeling the warmth of her touch and wanting to lie back and maybe sleep a little. "You know how we're the same?"

"No," I said.

"I don't think we're as guilty for the bad things we do. I think we're only a little guilty. I think, to tell you the truth, that we're mostly innocent. I'm not saying that you ran him over on purpose, kiddo. I'm just saying that if you did, I think it was a fair thing to do. He deserves to get a little bit of what he gives. That's all."

I leaned into her, closed my eyes, and let her hold me then. "That's okay," I said. I felt like a small kid again, as if I were seven or eight and everything would be done for me. "It was an accident. I slipped."

Ten minutes later, I was on the pay phone down the hall, trying to find a way to tell my mother that I was going to be more than a little bit late.

"Where the hell are you?" she asked. My mother was the sort of woman who rarely used words like that.

"I hurt him," I said. "He's getting stitches. There's going to be a scar." I could hear the relatives conversing in the background.

She didn't seem to hear a word of what I'd just said. "We're having dinner right now and you're missing it." Then, in a tone of exhaustion, she said, "He's going to get away with this, isn't he?"

I didn't say anything.

"I'm sorry, Malcolm," she said. "Sometimes I just want you to hate him as much as I do."

"Sure," I said, feeling ashamed because I didn't and never would hate him that way.

Beaty was wrong about my father. He didn't seem to need anybody's sympathy that night. He sat up straight behind the wheel, turned on the radio, and held an ice pack to his chin with one hand and drove with the other. The canyon road had a dangerous black sheen in the headlights and the radio warned of icy conditions, but none of this worried him, and we drove down the mountain without incident. The sky was clear and a hard, winter color of blue, in which the stars shimmered like foil. Below us was the flickering grid of the Salt Lake City valley, with the partial disk of the moon directly above it. Beaty had fallen asleep and curled into my father's shoulder. I could hear her soft breathing beneath the sounds of the radio. My father put the ice pack down now and touched his chin.

"Does it hurt?" I asked.

"It hurts enough," he said.

Then he said, "So what did your mom have to say?"

I looked over at my father now in the dark cab and said, "She said that she loved me but that that didn't mean she had to keep forgiving you. She said she would leave that up to me, if I wanted it." I didn't know where I'd gotten those words, since they weren't hers.

My father handed me his lighter and leaned over toward me in the dark with a cigarette in his mouth that he couldn't light on account of Beaty sleeping on him. When I lighted it, the soft orange flame uncovered Beaty's face and she stirred a little and seemed prettier in that light than she usually seemed.

"I'm sorry," he said. He took a long suck at his cigarette and the inside of the windshield glowed a hot orange.

"For what?" I said.

"About today. About blowing up at you. Let's just call it an accident, all right?"

"All right," I said.

He looked at me then. Behind the charcoal of his cigarette, I could see the coarse pattern the sutures made in his chin. "I'm sorry that you're going to be late."

"That was an accident," I reminded him.

"I'm still sorry," he said.

I didn't remember my father ever apologizing for something beyond his control, and I knew then that he was concerned that I love him and not hate him. He must have understood that it was my choice, that I could do either, and that my hate could injure him in a way that maybe Beaty's or my mother's or any woman's hate could not.

"You want to smoke this cigarette with me, Malcolm?" he said now.

"I don't smoke," I told him.

"It's not just to smoke it. It'll be our peace pipe. How about it?" We had pulled out of the canyon now and were on the freeway, the road easy and flat, with lanes of reflectors stretching out for miles ahead of us, where the dark was shallow and silvery from the moon and from the city lights. He took his hand from the wheel and gave me the cigarette. It was the first time I would smoke and the first time I understood that my father would love me forever, as best as he could, anyway, which was better than he did with other people. I put the cigarette between my lips, startled because the filter was moist from his mouth—a sour, warm taste that Beaty must have taken into her own mouth whenever she kissed him. I thought of how she desired him then, desired him the way men and women desire one another— a kind of love I knew very little about except that it was dangerous, that people hurt one another and learned to hate because of it. I thought about that and I thought about how I felt safe with my father then, smoking for the first time, inhaling deeply, my eyes watering as I coughed up a lungful of burning smoke and as my father put his hand on my back and said, "Easy there, kid."

STEALING

When the boys' father came to pick them up at their mother's and take them for the day, he was not driving his green Ford truck, but a red Porsche that could not have been his. "What do you think, boys?" His voice was huge with aggression and enthusiasm and with a sudden love for himself. He was wearing his monkey suit from the garage where he worked and had the smell of metal tools and the strong flammable odors of oil and gas and gin on him.

Standing out on the lawn, the boys' mother was still wearing her pink nightgown, ripped and coffee-stained on the sleeves. It blew in the wind and made her look fragile and discarded, like a candy wrapper. "What do you think you're doing? That car's not yours. Boys," she said, "you're not going with your father today." But the boys were already in the car, their eyes looking out at the woman through the dark glass that was made for speed. When she advanced, their father pushed her and she tumbled over the burned yellow grass, and before she could stand again, the little green house had disappeared and the man and his sons were driving on the freeway toward the mountains above the city, then in and out of the tunnels that pierced the mountains, until the buildings and streets of the city were tiny, like sutures, in the valley below.

The interior of the car had an expensive, feminine smell, a light perfume of leather and freshness. As the man drove, he talked about the car as if it were a beautiful woman who needed him to do something great, something heroic for her. "Listen to her purr, boys," he said. "We're not going to let her down. We're going to give her all we got."

Their mother no longer loved the man. Both boys knew that, even the smaller one, who was not yet five. "Where are we going to, Daddy?" this one asked.

"Oh no you don't," the man said. "I'm happy! Happy!" He said the word as if hammering on it. "And I'm not going to let you sour pusses ruin my fun, you hear?"

The boys kept asking him that same question, but their father only answered them with the figures of their acceleration. "Ninety," he said. "One hundred. One hundred and ten. One hundred and thirty-five."

The speed pushed the boys back in their seats and pressed against their skins like a firm caress, a preparation or a warning for something painful that would soon come. The windows began to tremble and the car beneath them shook as the man held it in a turn and the mountains and the other cars fell behind them. They had passed the timberline and huge treeless lumps of snow rose above them.

"One hundred and sixty," he said. He looked over and back at the boys now, trying to hold his speed. "One hundred and sixty-five." His eyes were dipped inward and were a strange purple color of black. He seemed hungry. "You never went this fast before, did you? Did you?"

RETRIBUTION

I

In the fall, when her mother began dying, Rachel joined the yearbook committee at her Catholic high school and met her first boyfriend. His name was Rand and he was from Germany. Rand's northern complexion, blond hair, and arctic blue eyes were strange and out of place in Tucson, all red dirt and asphalt grids, big parking lots and little adobe houses. On the first meeting of the Our Lady of Lourdes Yearbook Committee, Mr. Marcosian, the U.S. history teacher and Yearbook Committee coordinator, stood up and said, "It's our job to catch the personality of this year. Okay, people. Any questions?" Rachel hated being called "people," hated the sound of that "job," and thought about dropping out right then. But she needed something to do in the hours after school in order to avoid too much time at her dying mother's bedside in the late afternoons. Besides, she had seen Rand, one of the boys on the layout committee, and knew she'd want to come back and look at him again.

It would take months for her mother to die. Months and months. Carol was her name, and she'd been sick for years. She'd recently given up on treatment and decided that she wanted to be at home now, surrounded by her family. Her family wasn't much—Rachel and Rachel's father, Peter. And in the afternoons, when Carol called Rachel to her bed and they talked, Rachel felt both scared and shy. Her mother's bed was huge and bloated with white comforters because she could become unbearably cold. Her father always made sure a vase on the bedside table was filled with fresh-cut flowers, so fresh that, at times, ants from the garden outside still climbed their stalks. On the wall opposite her mother was a small oil painting done by her mother's mother, a woman whom Rachel had never met because she'd died in her fifties from the same kind of cancer that was killing Rachel's mother. In the painting, a small boat sailed out to sea. "I wonder where the boat is going. I wonder what my mother was thinking when she painted that boat," Carol said one afternoon.

"I don't," Rachel said. This question didn't bother her because the painting was so poorly executed that it had no perspective, no illusion of distance or space, no place to go. You just saw the flatness of the canvas and the obvious fact that the boat was going nowhere, that the boat was stuck forever in a bad painting.

"I sometimes make up stories about where it's going. I sometimes imagine that I'm sailing in it, that I'm twenty years old again, and that I can take only three or four of my most valuable possessions with me to a deserted island."

"Oh," Rachel said, "that scenario."

"I'd take you along," she said, smiling. "You'd be one of the three."

"You said possessions," Rachel said. "I'm a person."

"You're a difficult person," her mother said. Then her mother looked at her with a familiar expression, which meant she had some motherly advice. "Why don't you try wearing a little lipstick sometime. You'd be really pretty with a little color."

"I'm only fifteen," Rachel said. "I'm too young to worry about being pretty." She wished they weren't having this discussion. Her mother, as Rachel could remember and could still see from photographs, had been a beautiful woman before the treatment had mostly destroyed her looks. Her face had caved in; her hair had fallen out. She wore a scarf over her yellowing skull and had a woman come every Wednesday and Friday to draw eyebrows on her face and do her eyes. "Besides," Rachel added, "the nuns at school don't allow it."

"Nuns," Carol said, shaking her head. "I wasn't so easily dissuaded when I was fifteen. We used to put lipstick on right after school and wipe it off just before getting home, so that our parents wouldn't know."

"I don't care about being pretty," Rachel said.

"You know," her mother said, "teenagers are allowed to be a little bad sometimes, to be a little rebellious."

"That's okay. I don't need to act like that," Rachel said. But she became suddenly curious about her own mother then. "Did you smoke and stuff as a girl? Cigarettes, I mean. Behind the school building?"

Her mother smiled. "I don't think I should say." Then she took a drink of water and seemed to change her mind. She was still looking at the boat in the painting. "It was the sixties when I was a girl, and all the fun was just beginning."

"Maybe I don't want to hear this," Rachel said.

"Well," her mother said, "let's just say that maybe I smoked a little. Just a little. I didn't do anything dangerous."

"You had boyfriends?" Rachel asked.

"Sure," she said. "I had a few in my time. I was a pretty

girl and very vain. No one was good enough for me. You know the type?" her mother asked. She was studying Rachel again, examining her face. "If you ever want to borrow some lipstick, Rachel, you're welcome to go into my bathroom and take some."

"No," Rachel said. "I don't think so."

"It's in the second drawer down. People like pretty girls. They get away with an awful lot, you know."

"No," Rachel said again.

Her mother closed her eyes then for a long while in order to concentrate. It was pain, Rachel knew. It sometimes sneaked up on her and made her incapable of anything other than feeling it, fighting against it. Her mother's hand reached out of the covers and grabbed Rachel's arm, as if holding on, and Rachel, not wanting to see the inwardness, the aloneness of her mother's face, looked away and out the window, where the sunlight was broken into leafy patches by the orange trees in the backyard. She heard the roar of a Weed Eater. A bird. Someone shouting in Spanish. Her mother's grip tightened, then released. "Gone," her mother said. "Better." She and Rachel looked at each other as if nothing had happened. They never spoke of the cancer, of the pain. "So what three things would you take to your deserted island?" her mother asked.

Rachel thought about that question, and when not one thing occurred to her, she said, "I'm fifteen. How am I supposed to know?"

Rachel was on the photography staff for the yearbook and had been given the duty of following the sports teams, a task she hadn't volunteered for. At the assignments meeting, Mr. Marcosian had just looked up from the piece of paper in his hand and directly at Rachel and said, "How about you, Rachel, for sports teams?"

Matt Lieberman, a senior who had done sports for the last two years, made noises of complaint. "That's my job," he said.

"Let Matt do it," Rachel said.

"I'd like a girl to do it for a change," Mr. Marcosian said.

The only girl on the photography staff, Rachel wanted to turn it down. She hated all the cruelty and prestige associated with sports, and all the big, stupid boys who did them. But she also hated to be the center of attention, and twenty other people were staring at her then. "Okay," she said.

Her first assignment was the cheerleading squad, fourteen girls, mostly juniors and seniors, whom she found one rainy day after school building themselves into a human pyramid in the Our Lady auditorium, with blue mats spread out beneath them. "Who are you?" Julie Turly asked. Julie Turly was the squad captain and had just attained the peak of the pyramid, balancing herself carefully on the backs of a dozen other girls. She was a beautiful blonde who drove a white convertible Rabbit. Her father was a plastic surgeon. He did breast enlargements, Rachel had heard. And Julie herself was rumored to have performed group sex with Jeff Montoya and Tony Green, two linebackers on the football team. Cruel. So cruel what people said about others. Group sex. What would you do with more than two people? What would just two people do with each other? Rachel hadn't even kissed a boy. At the same time, she didn't like these girls and almost hoped the rumor was true. "I'm from the yearbook," Rachel said, pointing to the camera around her neck.

"Smile, girls," Julie said.

As soon as she got behind the camera, Rachel began to enjoy herself. This was one of the strangest objects she'd ever photographed: a living pyramid of the school's most beautiful and popular girls, dressed in red and gold, the colors of Our Lady, all smiling fakely, bulging eyes and stretched facial muscles betraying their real strain. "Hurry up, please," Julie said through her smile.

"A few more," Rachel said just when Christi Howard screeched, then screamed from the bottom of the pyramid, and the sky rained red miniskirts and white sneakers as the girls, Humpty Dumpty–like, came tumbling down.

Two days later, when Rachel developed her first roll of black-and-white film, these last pictures, she felt, were small masterpieces. They showed the girls broken down over the mats, on their stomachs, their backs, or on all fours, hands cupping the places that hurt most. Rachel overexposed their faces a bit, making them glow a bone-colored white, and touched up the dark backdrop of the auditorium until it became primitive and sepia-colored, until it shone black like night against a pane of glass, and Rachel's squad of cheerleaders transcended their stupid teenage vanity in a ghostly chromatism, in which the viewer could barely see that Julie Turly was Julie Turly, that Christi Howard was Christi Howard, that Samantha Woolsey was Samantha Woolsey. They were all just black-and-white figures wearing miniskirts, hobbled and apparently in terrible pain. It was spooky, very spooky, and Rachel was pleased.

"Look at these," she said to Rand, who was still in the yearbook office, working on the computer, when she emerged from the darkroom. This was the first time she'd spoken to the quiet, skinny blond boy with tender acne and thick horn-rimmed glasses, who for some reason had caught her eye again and again.

"Ouch," he said. *"Das schmerzt."*

"What's that mean?"

"It means that it hurts them."

"Funny way to talk," she said.

"I am coming from Germany," Rand said, his face flushing red.

"I didn't mean funny. I meant different. I meant"—she felt herself straining—"nice. I'm going to start off the sports section with this one and call it *The Agony and the Ecstasy: Girls Feel Pain, Too!*"

"What's agony and ecstasy meaning?"

"Extreme pain and extreme pleasure," Rachel said.

She saw from his eyes, watery and magnified behind his thick lenses, that he was thinking. *"Die Qual und die Ekstase."*

"Sure," Rachel said. "I guess."

He wrote the words down in a small notepad. "Thank you," he said, as if Rachel had genuinely given him something. "Agony and ecstasy," he repeated.

"Agony and ecstasy," Rachel repeated after him.

He looked at her picture again. "Why ecstasy?" Rand asked. "I don't see ecstasy. I only see agony."

Rachel looked for herself and could only concede. "Yep," she said.

Mondays and Wednesdays were gory, bloody days. They were driver's education days. After school let out, Rachel would sit in a darkened room with other sophomores and juniors, including the German boy, Rand, and view the graphic footage of car accidents, which was supposed to scare her into driving safely for the rest of her days. She saw bodies decapitated by steering columns, heads bashed into red mush by dashboards, limbs shorn and oddly lying in shattered glass on the roadside. "Hamburger films," she'd heard one girl call them. "Fast food." They showed survivors, too: mothers screaming and holding their faces in the white halls of hospitals, a boy weeping into the camera that zoomed in on the burn scabs on his face, then on the bandaged stump of his right arm as he said, wiping away the tears with his remaining hand, "I was drunk. I never, never should have been driving."

One day in the darkened room, Rachel grabbed Rand's hand and held on. He had hands, after all—fingers intact—and so did she. He seemed to stiffen, then relax, and Rachel felt him turn and look at her. But she stared at the screen, captivated, disgusted. "He was my son, my only son," a woman said, suddenly unable to speak for grief. Paramedics pounded a needle into the bloody sternum of an accident victim. They beat at his stopped heart with fists. The camera fled upward, away from the scene and into a darkness gouged with the strobing shadows of red and blue from the emergency vehicles below. The lights came on and Mr. Bobs, the driver's ed instructor and one of the assistant football coaches, stood in front of the class with his football whistle around his neck and his small flinty eyes shining black in the too-sudden fluorescent brightness. He blew on the whistle, and Rachel and Rand and forty or so other students gripped their ears. "Stupidity is death," he said. "If you think you can outsmart death by being stupid on the road, then you really are stupid."

"Jesus," somebody whispered behind Rachel.

Everyone seemed to agree that Mr. Bobs was more or less despicable, with his whistle and his red coach's pants and his super-short haircut, through which his pale scalp shone. He had a bony, bladelike face and wore the sort of small goatee that was popular now with the Our Lady boys and made the juniors and seniors who could grow one look slick and a little satanic, though it just made Mr. Bobs look boyish: a forty-five-year-old adolescent with a pointy spot of hair on his chin. He was horny, too. Rachel was sure that he stared at her breasts during her Wednesday driving lessons, though he pretended to be looking at her hands on the wheel, her feet on the pedals. "Good," he'd say. "Excellent." Adjectives that had really been meant, she knew, for her tits.

"All right, people," Mr. Bobs said now, "close your eyes. Eyes closed and heads down on your desks. Every last one of you." Behind him was a huge chalky blackboard, above which the bland white face of a wall clock with a red second hand sweeping slowly around was the last thing that Rachel saw before sealing her eyes. "Now," he said, "I want you to imagine your own funeral. The guests, the priest who christened you, the family friends, the aunts and uncles." He paused, then said in a fierce whisper, "Your mother. I want you to take a good long look at her. I want you to see exactly what she's wearing. Maybe the earrings you gave her one Christmas. Maybe the silly necklace you bought her for Mother's Day, the one she wears once or twice a year just to be polite or just because she loves you. I want you to be inside her head and feel exactly what she feels as she weeps over your coffin. Do it, people!"

He paused, and Rachel could hear his breathing, heavy and persistent, as if he'd just climbed a flight of stairs. The fact was, Rachel told herself, that Mr. Bobs was just sharing his torment with them. He was a freshly injured man and not the loud, hard soldier he pretended to be as he stood in front of the class. His wife, Mrs. Judy Bobs, a former English teacher at Our Lady, had fallen in love last spring with Mr. McGuan, the then Our Lady principal. They had fled the school in a bustle of controversy and were said to be living together in California somewhere. Now he was a small, hurt, horny, abandoned man, whose only solace in life was to stare at girls' breasts and to torture and frighten the kids in his driver's ed class. "One stupid, selfish prank from you means a life of loss for her," he said. Rachel refused to think of these things. Instead, she pictured inside the warm, velvety interior of her head absolutely nothing, a dark void, over which she saw the needle of the clock sweeping round and round as she tried not to let Mr. Bobs's words—*dead, mother, funeral, coffin*—puncture that deep black covering. But finally she could not resist seeing herself at her mother's funeral, herself in a baggy white T-shirt and a pair of oversized jeans, looking a little formless in her too-big adolescent clothes, which her mother hated so much. Rachel wouldn't even look pretty at her own mother's funeral, though Carol wouldn't be there anymore to say what she always said: "You're hiding yourself. You have a nice figure. I can tell you do behind all those clothes. But nobody else can. Nobody can see how nice you are, sweetie." It would be raining, of course, and her father would stand beside her in his dark suit, sobbing in the sloppy and terrible way that men do when they cry, loud and snotty and gasping for air. Rain water would fall from his matted bangs. Daddy, she'd want to say, but wouldn't. She would not cry. Not one tear. Not one, she promised herself.

"Okay," Mr. Bobs said. "Open your eyes now." When Rachel did, she had to squint at the brightness, and all she saw was Mr. Bobs, stupid Mr. Bobs, saying, "I hope you learned something. I hope you all now have a small idea of the pain you could cause."

————

After the gory films and after the stupid lecture, Rachel and Rand walked outside Our Lady and sat over on the grass, still holding hands. "Gross," Rand said. "Those films. I'm feeling sick in my stomach."

Gross was a word Rachel had taught him just yesterday. Rand was a fast learner. "You didn't really imagine it, did you? What Mr. Bobs told us to imagine."

"I couldn't not," Rand said.

"Your coffin and everything?"

Rand was picking clumps of grass out of the ground. "Not a coffin. I want to be burned and put in a jar. What is it called in English?"

"An urn," Rachel said, hating this conversation.

"An urn," Rand said. "My mother was crying over my urn. And you?"

"I was just in a coffin," Rachel said, lying. "A big, stupid black coffin. It was raining."

"Yeah," Rand said, "I know."

"Were there flowers at yours?" she asked.

"I don't think so," he said. Then he seemed sure. "No. No flowers. Just my parents and two really old grandmothers I don't know very well. And yours?"

"Sure. Lots of flowers. I hate that man," Rachel said. But she was already thinking about something else. "What if you could watch those hamburger films without being scared? If you could just do that, you might learn something. Not about driving, but about death." She was thinking about a boy in one of the films who had been cut out of a VW Bug with the Jaws of Life. He'd emerged bathed in blood, with his eyes wide open, glazed, and just looking at the world, seeming, Rachel thought, to have apprehended something beyond the mess of bent metal and screams and pain. Calm, hugely round eyes.

"You are not scared at the films?" Rand asked.

"Yes," Rachel said, "I'm scared. Definitely scared. But if I weren't..." Then she said, "Do you believe that God exists?"

"I believe that the man can't know this," Rand said.

"That's a funny kind of faith," she said. A hot wind that smelled of rain and fresh asphalt rose up. In the distance, a thunderstorm darkened the sky. Fall in Tucson often meant sudden, violent afternoon storms. "I hate people," Rachel said. "I don't think I can hate people and still believe in God, can I?"

"Maybe not," Rand said. "But I don't think you are hating people, really."

"Mr. Bobs," she said. "I hate him. He's a horny bastard, you know. He looks at me in the car during driving lessons."

"Horny?" Rand asked.

"That means he wants it all the time."

"It?" Rand asked.

"It," Rachel said.

"Oh," Rand said.

Rachel unzipped her backpack and took out a small black canister of Mace she'd taken from her mother's bathroom drawer the other day. Her mother had always worried about certain kinds of men and had carried this when she was still well enough to leave the house. "This is for Mr. Bobs," she said. "It's tear gas or something. If he tries anything..." She pretended to spray it into the air in front of her. "Bang," she said. "I hate him."

"God," Rand said. "I'm not sure. Tear gas. That seems..." His English failed him and Rachel saw that he was worried, maybe even a little scared.

"I probably won't ever use it," she said, putting the black

canister away. Poor worried Rand, she thought, lifting his hand and placing it on her cheek, where its warmth seemed immense. His hand smelled of pencil lead and wood shavings. A schoolroom smell. The smell of a smart boy, a fast learner. A boy who could never die, who could never just be ashes in a jar. Never. She kissed him right below the knuckles then—their first kiss—and felt the small, rapid panic of her heart.

"See," Rand said. His face was red and he was smiling. "You aren't really hating people, are you?"

"Maybe not," Rachel said. They felt the first large raindrops—one, two, three—big and wet and warm, before it began to pour all at once and they had to run for shelter.

But Rachel did hate Mr. Bobs. She hated him for his black mind and for undressing her with his eyes as she drove. There were always three student drivers in the car, but the other day—the day after which Rachel had decided to carry her mother's Mace—he'd dropped these students at their houses first, so that Rachel and Mr. Bobs were alone together. "Signal now," Mr. Bobs ordered. He had a deep robotic voice. "Good," he said. "Now ease into the turn." He wore large sunglasses with mirrored lenses—the kind that state troopers wore. They hid his eyes behind icy glass, so that Rachel could only feel his gaze on her and not see it. At times, when she knew he was staring at her, Rachel would look right at him until he said, "Eyes on the road, Rachel. Eyes on the road." As they turned on to Presidio that afternoon, one of Tucson's busiest streets, Rachel felt them again, Mr. Bobs's eyes probing deep inside her loose T-shirt while cars rushed by on both sides of the little Ford Taurus. A huge purple Cadillac in front of her had AMJAM on the license plate, and the pulsing bass of hip-hop reverberated from its insides. "What's AMJAM mean?" Mr. Bobs asked her. "That a rock group? A kind of music?"

"I don't know," Rachel said, still feeling him, his slimy, wet eyes inside her shirt.

"You like music? The Clash?" he said. "Nirvana? The Stones?" He turned on the radio then. "How 'bout this new guy, Kid Rock?"

"No," Rachel said, watching the driver of the Cadillac bob his head to the music. "I don't like that stuff much." And this was the truth: All that distortion and screaming had never done anything for her.

He turned the radio off. "Oh," he said. He moved in his seat. Something was strange, something was wrong, and all Rachel could do was look at the road, watch the light change from red to green, and think, Please, please just let him go away, as she accelerated through the inter-section.

"You're a quiet girl," Mr. Bobs said. "You're a loner, aren't you?" Rachel glanced over at him and saw that he was tapping his fingers on the dash and that one of his knees was motoring up and down, up and down. He was nervous. "Could I tell you something?" he asked. Rachel didn't say anything. She just drove. "I'd like to tell you that I think I understand how difficult it must be for you right now."

"Nothing's difficult," Rachel said.

"With your mother's illness," Mr. Bobs said. He cleared his throat, a terrible, snotty racket. "My mother died some two years ago."

"My mother," Rachel said, "is not ill." This was her secret and she had told no one at Our Lady about it.

"She died of cancer, too," Mr. Bobs said. "My mother did."

"My mother is not dying," she nearly shouted.

"I'm sorry," Mr. Bobs said. "I just wanted you to know that if you needed to . . . to talk . . ." He touched her shoulder then, softly, and Rachel turned and saw herself doubled in the bright silver plates of Mr. Bobs's glasses where she gripped at the steering wheel with both hands. "Okay?" Mr. Bobs's mouth said. She did it then—slammed the brake pedal to the floor with all her might. Mr. Bobs screamed. His glasses flew off and hit the windshield. Cars roared by, honking, and a huge Tucson Transit Authority bus screeched to a stop right behind them. The bus driver shook his fist at her. "Jesus God," Mr. Bobs yelled. Rachel started to drive again, while her teacher took deep, steadying breaths. "Why'd you do that?" he asked.

"I confused the brake with the gas, I guess," Rachel said.

His face looked naked and smaller without the glasses. "We almost died," he said. "Do you realize that we almost died? For crying out loud, kid, why are you smiling?"

She couldn't help it. It was a combination of his fear, his panic, his smallness, and the fact that he was right—they had almost died. They'd come within a hair's width, as her mother would say. "But we didn't," she said.

"Didn't what?" Mr. Bobs seemed to be shaking.

"We didn't die," she said.

II

No one liked her pictures. It was true: Their vision was dark and they seemed to record a large ratio of accidents and mishaps at the school sporting events. But Rachel could hardly be blamed. She'd simply and consistently found herself at the wrong place at the wrong time. At the first practice of the varsity basketball team, James Wood, the center, went up for a dunk and came down funny on his ankle. Rachel had been there behind the camera, so she snapped the picture of him cradling his right arm and hopping on one leg for the sideline. Then Blake Reems on the tennis team had been swatted so hard on the head by his doubles partner's aluminum graphite Prince racket that he'd hobbled to the fence and gripped the little chain links in order to stay on his feet. And finally, Linda Rose, a swimmer, had begun to climb out of the pool after winning the two-hundred-meter freestyle event, when she blacked out and oozed back into the water, her eyes closed and her face in utter and eerie peace.

"Interesting," Mr. Marcosian said, looking at her photographs at the quarter-year meeting of the photography staff. "Hmm." Mr. Marcosian was a short man with thinning ashy gray hair and small, quick eyes of a freakish, bunny rabbit blue. He wore brown corduroys and a brown cloth necktie almost every day, and said "interesting" and "hmm" a lot in his history classes, digging his fingers into his slight beard. "Aren't we winning?" he said. "Aren't there pictures of cheering and victory and such to take?"

And such? Rachel hated words at times. "I didn't make these things happen," Rachel said.

"Of course not," Mr. Marcosian said. "But isn't photography about selection, about finding what we want to see and recording it?"

"I didn't select these things. They were just there. They found me. They selected me." These words scared her. They seemed true.

At home, she showed the photographs to her mother, who felt well enough that afternoon to sit up in one of the living room armchairs and watch through the window as the afternoon storm darkened the sky. "Oh," her mother said, holding up two of Rachel's pictures. "What happened to this poor girl?" It was Linda Rose, the swimmer, her eyes closed, her face in that deep, strange peace.

"She passed out," Rachel said. "It was kind of weird. She'd just won, and while everybody's cheering, she closes her eyes and sinks to the bottom of the pool. Her mother actually jumped in with her clothes on. It was scary. But Linda was okay afterward."

Carol said "Hmm" at the picture, just as Mr. Marcosian had.

"I want you to like them," Rachel said.

"I don't, I'm afraid," she said, putting them down. "I like that you did them. But I don't much care for them."

"Great," Rachel said. "Thanks."

"Why would anyone take pictures like these?" her mother asked.

"God," Rachel said. "Please don't ask me that. That's exactly what Mr. Marcosian thought." She felt herself hating Mr. Marcosian then, the small man digging in his little gray beard for insights. She pictured spraying the tear gas in his blue rabbit eyes, making him claw at his face and weep. He wouldn't be saying "interesting" then. "Mr. Marcosian wants pictures of victory and cheering."

"Sure," her mother said. "I can understand that."

"Fatuous," Rachel said, a word she'd recently learned from a novel she was reading in English class. "Empty high school rhetoric."

"Nice word," her mother said, putting her head down on the chair and looking out the window at the storm, where a streak of lightning illuminated the sky, followed by a delayed rumbling that seemed to get beneath the house and shake it. "I like a good thunderstorm."

"You're avoiding me," Rachel said. "You won't even have an argument with me."

"I'm tired," Carol said. She closed her eyes for a moment, then, too slowly, opened them again and turned to look at Rachel, who noticed the extreme thinness of her mother's neck, the cords pushing against the white, white skin. "I wish you'd wear nicer shirts." She pulled on a loose fold of Rachel's T-shirt. "Don't you have nice blouses? Maybe your father needs to take you shopping."

"I don't want to go shopping with Dad."

"And a little makeup, too. You haven't forgotten where my lipstick is?"

"You're a broken record," Rachel said. But her mother didn't seem to hear her or care to hear her. More lightning flashed and the rain started coming down, and Rachel's mother closed her eyes again and seemed about to fall asleep. "What if I told you," Rachel said, considering every word carefully now, "that one of my teachers at Our Lady wanted to sleep with me, wanted to have sex with me?"

Her mother sat up in her chair and looked at her. The shadows in the room were riddled by the downpour and fell in dark streaks down Carol's face. "I'd say that either you're choosing the wrong way to get my attention, or that you'd better go get your father and set up an appointment with Father Kelsh right this minute." Father Kelsh was the Our Lady principal.

Rachel looked out the window. "I'm making it up, I guess."

"Rachel," her mother said in a tone that meant she'd better look at her. Rachel did this. "Don't, please, do that. Don't say that sort of thing."

"I'm rebelling now. You said I was allowed to."

"Ridiculous," her mother said in a harsh, disciplinarian

voice that Rachel remembered from her childhood and had
not heard in years.

"You don't think I'm pretty," Rachel said.

Carol smiled. "Of course I do." Then she said, "I'm tired,
Rachel. I wonder if you'd give me some time."

Rachel found her father in the kitchen. "Mom thinks I'm
ugly," she said.

"Your mother's tired, kiddo."

" 'Kiddo'?" she said. "I'm not exactly a kid anymore."
She and her father hadn't seen each other much lately. Last
year, between working and spending time with her mother
at the hospital, he'd almost never been home. And now that
he worked only part-time at his bank and was around the
house again, he'd call her things like "kiddo," though he
mostly just sat in his large chair in the living room or in
his study with the lights off and said nothing. All the same,
she loved him, his round, soft face and mostly bald head,
loved him so much that it had been hard for her, when she
first went to high school, to find the skinny, bony-faced boys
with all their hair at all attractive. "Daddy," she said.

"Yes," he said. His necktie was loosened and he'd just
made himself a drink. But his eyes were red. He'd been
crying in here, she knew, and he'd stopped for her and
wouldn't mention it. Everyone in this house did their crying
alone, and Rachel guessed that she liked it best that way.

"How's the bank?"

"The bank's the bank," he said.

"School's school," she said, even though he hadn't asked.
She dropped her photographs on the table in front of him.
"Nobody likes my pictures."

He tried to rescue her then. "I do," he said.

"Not very convincing," she said.

"They're art pictures, I'd say. Not easy to understand. Challenging to the viewer."

"Wrong," she said. "They're sports pictures. They're for the Our Lady yearbook. I'm the sports photographer."

"Sports photographer?" he said. He'd obviously assumed she was joking.

"Yeah," she said. "Sports is my big hobby. I love sports." There was a long silence between them. More lightning flashed outside and the kitchen windows ran with gray water and the rain came down still harder, a thousand million tiny explosions pummeling the roof overhead, and they didn't know what to say to each other. "You told my teachers about Mom," she said. "You told them and you didn't tell me you were going to. Why'd you do that?"

"We thought it might be easier on you that way. We knew you wouldn't want us to, but we thought it best."

"Well," Rachel said, "it's not easier."

Her father took a sip of his drink and stared into it as he spoke. "We'd like you to see someone, Rachel."

"A shrink?" she asked.

"Sort of."

"Why doesn't Mom ask me?"

"Your mother's sick." His voice became almost angry.

"What if I say no?"

"We'd rather you not say no."

Rachel looked down at her feet, at her big, blue Nikes. "No," she said.

When Rachel needed to cry, she retreated after school to the far stall in the basement girls' bathroom, which was almost always empty. Once locked into her stall, she cried out loud and heard her voice, mournful, hollow, angry, amplified in that strange, cold echo chamber. After blowing her nose and calming herself, she'd start again, this time louder, more ferociously, until she had exhausted herself. Sometimes she'd flush the toilet beneath her so that the roar of the water would muffle the moans of her own voice. Rachel hated public rest rooms, but they seemed like the right place for grief: dirty, semiprivate, shameful places, smelling of chemicals and urine.

Afterward she'd sit on the toilet and read the graffiti, which was especially graphic because, only three years ago, Our Lady had been an all-boys Jesuit school, and due to limited funding, many of the girls' rooms had been left as is, with the arcane and mostly disgusting signs of boys everywhere. Along the walls, a row of urinals, rusted and now dry, remained, the strange presence of which always summoned in Rachel's mind a line of boys facing the wall, legs spread execution-style, the seats of their pants baggy and hitched on their skinny hips as they held their penises like water pistols and aimed at the little silver-latticed drains, and maybe spit or pulled a pen from their crotch pocket to write, "Keep your eyes up here, hand master!" *Hand master.* She didn't know exactly what one was, but the dark suggestion of greedy and obsessive masturbation didn't escape her, and it made her giggle through her drying tears.

And looking at the scratched aqua-blue door of her stall and the dividers on both sides of her, she read dozens of other disgusting predatory markings naming girls who were either fictitious or had come from the old sister school, St. Mary's High, across the street from Our Lady, where Rachel's mother had been a student. "Linda Crotch likes it up the butt," she read. She studied a small illustration of a jovial penis, a large grin drawn across its snakelike face. It thought to itself in a balloon drawn above, "Boy, would I like some pussy." "Kindra lets me come in her cunt," another message read, accompanied by a faded sketch of the cunt itself, an inky hole surrounded by curly hair. And as Rachel sat on the toilet urinating or as she stood, her panties pulled down around her knees, changing her pad, she felt a little sick to her stomach. Surrounded by pictures of erect penises and open vaginas, she'd wipe herself and pull her panties up with the tips of her fingers, not wanting to touch her own messy self and thinking of Mr. Bobs, his glasses, his thin, sucked-in cheeks, the fact that he had touched her, if only on the shoulder. Did he think of Rachel's vagina, her cunt, her hole? Even her mother, her dying body now shrunk to almost nothing, had smiled at her, remembering boyfriends, and said, "Sure. I had a few in my time." Rand had a penis, a scrotum, and he must, behind his sweet smile, his funny and pure foreign accent, have felt this way. And Rachel herself, reading these strange messages, had wondered what it would be like to sit down on a cock and hold it deep inside her. She'd hurry to leave then, exit the stall, wash her hands thoroughly, at least twice, with too much pink soap from the dispensers, and rush outside, where, trying to forget her thoughts, she'd board a city bus home or, on Wednesdays, get into Mr. Bobs's car.

So it was hard for Rachel to understand why she did what she did on that Wednesday afternoon after her father had asked her to see a shrink. First, she flushed away the toilet's yellow contents, then asked out loud, just to make sure, "Is anyone in here?" before she leaned off the seat and, thinking of Mr. Bobs's black mind, of Mr. Marcosian's dislike of her pictures, of her mother's eyes half-closed before Rachel's dangerous words had brought her back to life, scribbled out her own dirty contribution: "Julie Turly sucks Mr. Bobs's big dick." She scratched "dick" out and, enjoying the improvement, wrote "cock." She read it back to herself, feeling now that this minor accomplishment would be her secret, her small, disgusting deed that she would keep from everyone else. She left the girls' room in a hurry then, without looking back and without washing her hands.

That afternoon, Rachel kept the small black canister of Mace close at hand in her right front pocket during Mr. Bobs's driving lesson. She remained attentive and always aware of where Mr. Bobs's eyes might be, though in the last weeks, since their near accident, Mr. Bobs's gaze no longer seemed to wander toward her. He had been all business since then, as he was that afternoon, repeating his usual axioms: "The best offense is a good defense" and "Anticipate, anticipate, anticipate" and "Always keep two car lengths between you and the driver ahead" and, in conjunction with that last one, "Fences make good neighbors, people!" and, finally, his favorite it seemed, "Stupidity on the road is death on the road." He'd even taken to dropping Rachel off first or second so that they were never alone in the car.

"Signal at least five seconds before turning," Mr. Bobs told Rachel, who had just made a sloppy turn in front of a tailgating Mustang. She saw his foot poised over the brake pedal on his side of the car. He was cautious, maybe even scared when she drove now.

"I'm out of it," Rachel said. "I'm a little sleepy today."

"Well then," Mr. Bobs said, "you're on your way to becoming a statistic."

"Sorry," Rachel said, feeling satisfied that she had annoyed him a little and feeling also the unfamiliar power of her secret over him, even imagining it as he sat next to her reciting his stupid platitudes: Mr. Bobs making the sounds of a sick animal as Julie Turly blew him, as Julie Turly reached up and grabbed the little silver whistle around his neck and pulled on its yellow cord until he came.

"Signal. Check your blind spot. Observe the five-second rule." They were driving toward Rachel's home now, up her quiet street. "A little sloppy today, Ms. White." She hated the fact that he'd just used her last name, the implication of her smallness ringing in the tone of his voice. She stepped out of the car and Jason Brown took her place. "See you on Monday." The stupid man didn't even look at her as he said this, as the car pulled away and Rachel thought about going inside, though she didn't. She couldn't sit at her sick mother's bed just then. So she stood on the curb and watched the blue Ford Taurus with the funny yellow beacon on its cab that said STUDENT DRIVER turn the corner and drive out of sight. *Male slut.* She'd heard a girl say that in the hall at Our Lady once. *Mr. Bobs is a male slut.* She thought about crying till exhausted and then writing those words on the dirty bathroom wall in letters so large and crooked that they'd make the bathroom scream with what Rachel felt inside her now. But everything was silent. It was four o'clock and the sun was full in the sky and Rachel's neighborhood was sleeping. The houses were shut up behind their lava-rock front yards and no one walked on the sidewalks. Rachel had a secret. At least she had that. She wondered, though, when Mr. Bobs might drop her off last again, when he might ask her about her taste in music, her quietness, her loneliness. She almost hoped he would ask her these things. And if he did, Rachel would be ready for him. She'd be ready for him because she hated Mr. Bobs, every disgusting, horny inch of him.

One day after school, Rachel went to Rand's house for dinner without telling her parents. Rand's mother and father talked rapidly to each other and to Rand in German, and it was a disappointing discovery for Rachel to hear Rand speak so easily, so proficiently in a language she could not understand. She missed his accent, his awkward speech rhythms, his dependency on her as a sort of dictionary. Now she was dependent on him. "What's that word mean?" she asked him.

"*Kartoffeln,*" he said, "means 'potatoes.' *Reichen Sie mir bitte die Kartoffeln,*" Rand said, trying to teach her how to ask for the potatoes to be passed.

But Rachel didn't want to learn. She wanted to understand things. "I can't say that," she said.

Rand's parents didn't look foreign at first. They just looked like people, like Americans to her. Mr. Taub still wore his work suit with his tie loosened, just as Rachel's father did after work, and a pair of fine wire spectacles that made his face appear angular and refined, maybe a little more European than American. Mrs. Taub wore blue jeans and a funny T-shirt with a pelican on it saying something in a language Rachel didn't recognize. "What's the pelican saying?" Rachel asked.

"That's Arabic," Mrs. Taub said. "It's saying 'Learn languages so that you can learn the world.'" Her accent was very strong and Germanic, as if the vowels were climbing up little slopes in each word she said. "It's an advertisement for the private language school I worked for in Tunis some years back."

"Oh," Rachel said. She'd never heard of Tunis and felt very alone and ignorant in her inability to see that strange city where Rand had once lived, when something terrible happened at the table. Mrs. Taub reached over with her napkin and wiped a bit of food from the corner of Rand's mouth—a typical motherly gesture. All at once, Rachel could not help but imagine this woman broken down and crying over her son's urn, his little jar of ashes. It would be raining, drizzling on two very old ladies. And there would be no flowers. Just Rand's jar. Mrs. Taub and all she knew would count for nothing then. Rachel looked at Rand, his soft, smart eyes, wet and bent funnily beneath the lenses of his glasses, as he forked a bite of potatoes into his mouth. She mourned a little bit for him. She wanted Mr. Bobs and his darkness out of her head.

"We are hearing many good things about you from Rand," Mrs. Taub said. "You are a photographer, Rand is telling us."

"No one likes my pictures," Rachel said. It somehow made her feel more secure to demean herself in front of Rand's European parents.

"Art is a matter of taste," Mr. Taub said. "There will be some who like your pictures, I'm sure." He spoke perfect English, with a surprisingly crisp British accent.

"Thank you," Rachel said, though she wasn't sure why she'd said that. To make things worse, she repeated it in German. *"Danke,"* she said.

"Very good," Mrs. Taub said, and Rachel felt incredibly stupid.

After dinner, Rachel called home and her father answered. "It's Rachel," she said.

"Hi," he said. He sounded tired and far away, as if he'd forgotten to speak directly into the receiver. Behind her, Rachel heard the clattering of plates and the strange sounds of German being spoken, and right then she felt that she was thousands of miles away in a foreign country; she missed her father, missed him terribly. "You don't know where I am," she said.

"I thought you were working on the yearbook or having your driving lesson."

"It's almost nine o'clock," Rachel said.

"Yes, it is," he said.

"Are you there?" Rachel actually said this, and it confused her, the way it had just come out like that. "Dad?" she said, and she felt her throat choking, her eyes tearing up, thinking about how, years ago, they used to play a game called Mr. Boo, a silly version of hide-and-seek. "Where is Mr. Boo hiding?" she'd call out as she searched for her father in the closets, under beds, in bathtubs, until she'd find him and scream, "There's Mr. Boo!"

"What?" her father said. "Sure I am." Then he finally realized what he should have already asked, "So where are you?"

"I'm at Stephanie's," Rachel said, feeling immediately disappointed by her lie. She'd wanted it to feel deceptive and maybe even a little malicious. But it was a useless lie. Rachel had nothing of any value to conceal from him, nothing that could make her seem as remote as her father now seemed to her. "Stephanie's a friend of mine," she said, though Stephanie didn't exist and her lie was clearly pointless. "What are you doing now?" she said. "Are you still in your work suit?"

He seemed to take a minute to look at himself. "I guess so," he said. "I'm just sitting here." Then he added, "Your mother's sleeping. She's fine."

"Yes," Rachel said, "I know. I'll be home soon." And then they hung up.

On the walls in Rand's bedroom were pictures of Rand at various ages and in various parts of the world. Working in some capacity for the German government, Mr. Taub had taken his family everywhere, it seemed. In one of the pictures, Rand, a bare-chested toddler with huge blue eyes, played with two older black boys on the dirt ground in the African Congo. In another, as a little boy, he wore a funny-colored hat and sat on a camel in the Sahara Desert. In another, Rand, older now, brought a piece of octopus to his mouth with a pair of chopsticks. Aside from the part of Mexico that bordered Tucson, Rachel had never been outside her country, and she found the images on Rand's walls overwhelming in the unexpected vastness of the world they showed. She hoped she would never have to eat octopus. She hoped she would never be half-naked in the Congo, surrounded by other half-naked children. But Rand had done these things. He seemed to know a great deal that she did not, and maybe somehow his knowledge could protect her.

But when she asked him one afternoon in his bedroom, "What's the world like, Rand?" he looked at her as if he were totally stupid, as if he knew nothing about the smart, quick-learning boy she had always believed him to be.

"I don't know," he said.

"Yes you do," she said. "You've lived everywhere."

"Okay," he said. "You are familiar with that song 'It's a Small World'?" Rachel nodded her head, thinking about that song, the chorus of children's voices that always sang it. "That," Rand said, "is a stupid song. It's not small. It's big. It's bigger than you could ever imagine. Nothing's the way you think."

"I didn't really want to hear that," Rachel said. Rand shrugged his shoulders and Rachel wished he were less truthful and more generous, more deceptive.

"It's a good kind of big, though," he said. "It shows you things you would never expect."

"I know that already," Rachel said.

That same afternoon, Rand and Rachel exchanged E-mails with a girl named Lisa who was spending the year with her family on a small island near the North Pole. Rand had a computer in his room and liked to E-mail German friends and other kids he'd met while living in far-off places. "E-mail," Rachel said. "I didn't know they had E-mail on the North Pole. Ask her what she did over the weekend. Ask her about polar bears and the animals there."

Five minutes later, they received her response: "We saw the polar ice caps yesterday and even had a freezing-cold picnic on one. The seasons are way extreme here. Right now, it's eleven o'clock at night and the sun is still shining bright. But in about a month, it will be pitch-black all day long. There are no penguins or white bears here. All that stuff's a lie."

"Oh," Rachel said. "I was sure there were at least penguins."

"I think that is the South Pole," Rand said.

"Maybe," Rachel said. She was picturing now the vast white emptiness in which Lisa and her family had picnicked, the plane of ice as far as you could see, the dead, colorless space there, and was realizing that Rand would eventually, sooner than later, leave again and live somewhere else, maybe even the North Pole. He would be swallowed up, and Rachel hated the world.

In the late fall, Rachel combed the sidelines at a football practice one day with her camera. The boys on the Our Lady football team had names like Billy Bat, Rat Swank,

Bob Knight, Mark Sword—names of animals and weapons and warriors. She expected to laugh at them in their funny tight pants. But she was awed instead by the persistent, repetitive violence they endured as they grouped off in separate packs along the field and ran what were called drills—passing drills, blocking drills, tackling drills, formation drills—most of which consisted of sprinting and footwork, and ended with one boy or several boys obliterating another. Leading these strange exercises, coaches in red pants shouted at the top of their lungs. At the end of one side of the field, Rachel was surprised to see Mr. Bobs not merely shouting but screaming, haranguing his group. "Ladies!" he shouted at them. "A bunch of ladies!" His boys faced off and exploded into one another. "Hit him! Hit him good! I want to hear it when you hit one another." Their helmets cracked again and again, and some boys tumbled backward and wriggled grotesquely in the grass before getting to their knees, then crouching and colliding again. Rachel prepared herself to see another accident, a boy who would not rise, a bloody nose, a pinched nerve, though none of this happened. Finally, it was Mr. Bobs who fascinated Rachel most—Mr. Bobs, who had spent, in his other capacity, most of the semester warning them against collision and who now blew his whistle to send whole columns of boys into a strange, controlled orgy of brutality. "Get down! Get down! And explode out of it!" His face was red and scribbled with bright streaks of sweat. Veins popped from his throat as he clamped down on the whistle, and Rachel turned her camera on him, thinking about how Mrs. Judy Bobs, a pretty blond woman who had taught Dickens and Jane Austen and Shakespeare in Rachel's English class last year, had driven off to California with Mr. McGuan, a better-looking man than Mr. Bobs, how she had left this poor furious man to grow a stupid little goatee, to stare at his girl students, and to scream at his football players. He was alone now, alone and yelling into thin air at the top of his lungs. Rachel wanted to do that. She wanted to scream like that at the top of her lungs. Scream and scream and scream. She snapped his picture again and again. She didn't know at first what she felt then for Mr. Bobs, this helpless grown man raging into nothing, though she thought it might be pity.

For a boy who had sat on camels in Tunisia and ridden on the roofs of train cars in India, for a boy who was supposed to know the world and would, Rachel knew, leave Tucson behind, Rand was terrible at love. He was slow and uncomprehending when Rachel finally made him sit on his bed, then bent over him and kissed him on the lips. He wouldn't close his eyes and he wouldn't take his glasses off, the cold, thick rims of which gouged at Rachel's cheeks. "I need them to see," he said, holding them on with both hands. When she blew in and nibbled at his ears, he could only giggle and squirm and struggle out of her arms. And he seemed completely baffled by Rachel's tongue. "It's what you do," she tried to explain to him. "People kiss with their tongues."

"I don't know," Rand said.

"Of course you do. Everybody knows that."

These were Rachel's first kisses, her first embraces, and she wanted them to count. She wanted to feel desired, ravished, and one afternoon, sitting Indian-style opposite Rand on his bed, she finally insisted. She pulled her T-shirt off and lifted Rand's hands to her breasts and put them over her bra. "Go ahead," she said. "Do it."

"Do what?" he asked. He didn't move his hands. They seemed stuck to her smallish breasts, glued there.

"Feel me up," she said.

"Feel up?" he said.

He didn't even understand the English, so she had to make it simple. "Love me," she said, after which Rand went mute and just stared at her. "Take your glasses off, Rand." His eyes looked so pathetic and worried behind his thick lenses that she finally reached over and removed them herself and hid them under the bed. He must have been frozen with fear, because he'd been unable to take his hands from her and defend himself.

"Please," he said. "I can't see." He squinted at her and finally did lift an arm and touch her face, softly, the way the blind do, trying to see with his fingers. "Where are my glasses, Rachel?"

"Kiss me," Rachel said, leaning into him, digging into his lips with hers, pushing a hand down and beginning to pull his belt loose.

"No please," Rand said. Spit came from his mouth, and when she kissed him now, she felt only his teeth. But her eyes were closed and she was reaching for his crotch, his cock, when he put his hands down and pushed her so forcefully away that she hit the wall behind her with a thud. Her chest felt hollow, as if the force of the impact had emptied her. He shouted out a word in German, a word full of panic and shock. His blond hair was a mess now, as if he'd come in from a windstorm, and his eyes shone with rage and tears and blindness. "Where are my glasses hiding? My glasses!" he shouted.

She got them for him, and when he put them on and could see her again, he seemed to hate her. "Leave," he said.

"I'm sorry," Rachel said.

"Out," he said. "Out."

When she got up to leave, he threw something at her. It was her shirt, and she picked it up from her feet, put it on, and left.

In the weeks before Christmas, Rand did not speak to her or even look at her at school. In the yearbook office, he'd sit staring at the computer screen even when she would pull a chair up next to him and say, "Hi, Rand. It's me, stupid. It's Rachel. Remember?" He'd just type away or maneuver the mouse. "How's Lisa on the North Pole?" she asked him. When he said nothing, she just sat there and noticed how the chilly blue light from the monitor seeped into Rand's face and made him look frozen and cruel, as if he'd already gone to one of the poles, to the farthest Arctic regions. "Happy holidays and stuff," she said before going away.

III

One evening Rachel fell asleep in the dark of her room, feeling sick to her stomach, feeling that she'd lost everything, feeling that hunkering down into darkness, into sleep, was her only way to find comfort now. When she woke the next morning, she looked out her window and saw what seemed to be a storm of purple confetti falling from the dark sky. She walked outside in her T-shirt and bare feet, shivering, seeing her breath turn to smoke in the cold air and tasting a crystal of ice on her lip. Snow. Snow in the desert. She'd never seen it, not in Tucson, and she ran down the hall to her mother's bedroom and woke her. "It's snowing," she said. Her mother, dressed in a simple white nightgown, woke very slowly, as if even this simple act hurt her, and Rachel seemed to have to wait a long time before her mother was ready to hear and understand what she now said again. "It's snowing outside. Look."

When Carol turned around and looked out the window behind her, she said, "Am I dreaming?"

"Do you want me to pinch you?" Rachel asked.

"Please don't," she said. Then her mother said, "Oh . . . oh," and pointed to her pills on the bedside table.

Rachel poured her water from a pitcher and her mother slowly swallowed three blue gel caps and closed her eyes, concentrating now on the terrible thing inside her. "Is the nurse coming soon?" Rachel asked. A nurse came now every day.

"In an hour," her mother said. Then she said, her eyes still closed and her head resting on her pillow, "Tell me about something."

"What?" Rachel hated herself for having nothing to say.

"Anything," her mother said. "Say anything."

"I have a boyfriend," Rachel said. "My first boyfriend."

Her mother actually smiled. "You've been keeping secrets from me," she said.

"His name is Rand. It's a funny name, I know, but it's German. He's German, from Germany. He speaks German and everything, and his father's a diplomat, which is why they're in Tucson instead of in Heidelberg. I guess I didn't want to tell anybody right away. I thought he might drop me."

"Why would you think that?" her mother asked. "I bet he really likes you."

"*Vielleicht,*" Rachel said. "That's German for 'perhaps.' "

"He's teaching you German?"

"I like him and everything," Rachel said. "But he's maybe

a little pushy sometimes. He wants to do things that I don't want to do yet."

"Things?" her mother said. She opened her eyes and kept them open. "What things?"

Rachel looked outside at the snow, each flake about the size of a grain of rice, and hated the particular way the truth had worked itself into her lies. She didn't want to hear this truth, but she said it anyway. "You know, sex things. But I'm not ready for that and I told him so, and he still seems to like me."

"Good," her mother said. "Good for you. Do we need to have a talk? Would you like to ask me some questions?"

"Not right now," Rachel said.

Her mother closed her eyes and smiled. "You're a strong girl, Rachel. Very strong."

Rachel looked out the window again at the strange snow that disappeared as soon as it hit the red dirt ground, the desert, in which it shouldn't have been snowing in the first place. "Lies have long legs," her mother had always told her. "They run away from you; they chase after you." But she'd never told Rachel how lonely lies were, how friendless and loveless they made you feel.

Her mother said, "I'm sure he'll be very nice once he calms down." Then she said with mock disgust, "Boys."

"Boys," Rachel said, agreeing.

On the last Wednesday before the semester break, Rachel put a small black tube of lipstick in her backpack and dressed in one of her mother's blouses, which she'd borrowed without asking and which fit her more snugly than anything Rachel owned. Looking in the mirror, she saw that her smallish breasts took on shape and she could just make out the white straps of her bra, the fine lattice of which made her feel both interior and exposed. As she walked through the brown hallways of Our Lady and took in their familiar smells of stinky tennis-shoe leather and pencil erasure, she felt herself distinctly being seen as if the eyes of boys—glancing quickly toward her and just as quickly away—had coated her in a second skin, a sheath of light and uncertain thoughts.

After school, she retreated to her stall in the basement rest room, peed, then wept as loudly as ever, after which she scrawled out an especially graphic message about the Our Lady principal and the director of religious studies. "Father Kelsh does Sister Mariam Anne doggy-style." *Does* seemed to her even more offensive than the word *fuck,* and she was pleased with what Mr. Cummins, her English teacher, would have called her word choice. But neither her cry nor her message seemed to do much for her that day. She stood from the toilet, pulled her panties up and her skirt down. She had just finished her period and so felt more solid now and less self-conscious in that murky, confused way. In front of the mirror, Rachel took out the black tube of lipstick, the name of which—Secret Rose—had made her think of dew, mists, and light, grainy rainfall, of moister climates than Tucson's. But there was nothing floral about this thick, substantial red, and as she stroked the color on, she seemed to be cutting into her own skin, exposing a soft, wounded depth that she had not guessed at. "Ouch," she said to herself in the mirror.

When she got into the backseat of the Taurus, Mr. Bobs, his sunglasses off, addressed her in the rearview mirror. "You're first, Rachel."

She told him right off that she had forgotten her house

key that day and that her parents wouldn't return home till later. "They're at the hospital." How easily that lie had come to her. "I thought maybe I could drive last today," she said to the slice of eyes and nose in the rearview mirror.

The eyes looked at her, considered her. "Okay," Mr. Bobs said, his face sliding out of the mirror, where instead she saw a slanted section of the backseat and of her own lap, where her hands, skinny and cut off at the wrists, lay. Then he readjusted the mirror.

Stacy Wallright drove first. She was a little pudgy and drove fearfully, so that Mr. Bobs had to repeat the same stern advice he always reserved for Stacy. "Driving afraid can be just as dangerous as driving recklessly. At the end of the day, the old lady going thirty-five in her Buick on the interstate and the teenager jumping train tracks in his Camaro end up in the same place." He cleared his throat. "Fear kills, too," he said.

Why did Mr. Bobs like to talk about death so often? Every time he mentioned it, he'd sit up straighter and puff with authority.

After dropping Stacy off, Jason Brown got behind the wheel. Jason Brown was what Mr. Bobs called an "overconfident" driver. His manner was lax, and today he cruised with the fingers of one hand draped over the wheel, so that Mr. Bobs had to say, "Two hands, Jason. Always two hands on the wheel. If you think you can avoid an accident with a couple of fingers, you're wrong."

Jason put his other hand on the wheel, though he was slow to do it and clearly felt that it clashed with his style.

Finally, after Jason Brown got out, it was Rachel's turn. Rachel had been labeled a "careless" driver by Mr. Bobs ever since she'd confused the brake for the gas that day, and as she eased into her first turn, she wanted to point out the care she'd just taken. "I followed the five-second rule this time," Rachel said.

"This is your last practice run," Mr. Bobs said. "After this, you're on your own."

"You ever been in an accident, Mr. Bobs?" Rachel asked. "I mean, with Our Lady students."

"No," he said. "Never."

"Probably the closest you came is with me that time." Mr. Bobs said nothing, and she felt herself achieving a nice hot contempt for this man who had been ignoring her now for weeks. "Guess what?"

Mr. Bobs didn't say anything to this, save for "Take a right turn on Mesa Drive."

"I took your picture a few weeks ago."

"My picture?" Mr. Bobs said. Rachel looked over at him, expecting him to engage her now, though he didn't. He faced straight ahead, with his large shieldlike glasses on, as if it would be dangerous for him to turn and look at her.

"On the football field last week," she said. "I'm the school sports photographer. You're going to be in the yearbook."

"All right," he said, "we'll take a few left-hand turns and then finish up."

"You seemed angry, the way you were shouting at those boys to hit one another. Are you angry, Mr. Bobs?" He took a deep, irritated breath. "Anyway, the way you were shouting made me think about something for some reason. I thought about Mrs. Bobs, about the way she left and everything, about how furious you must have been when she did that."

Mr. Bobs was looking at her now, though she couldn't know what was in his eyes—rage, shock—behind those silly glasses. "We're having a driving lesson," he said. "Not a conversation."

She hated the coldness, the indifference in his voice. She wanted him to be angry or hurt, to yell or cry. "The other week," she said, "we were having a conversation. We talked about what music I liked, about how lonely I seemed, about my mother."

"No," Mr. Bobs said, his voice still calm and chilly. "We didn't. I don't remember any such conversation."

"You touched me," Rachel said. "You put a hand on my shoulder."

"No," Mr. Bobs said. "I didn't." Then he said, "Take a right at this light."

"Sure," Rachel said, pulling into the left lane and taking a left turn onto a quiet residential street.

"I said right," Mr. Bobs said.

"No you didn't," Rachel said. "You said left. You said to take a left turn at the light."

"Take a right here and turn around," he said calmly, as if none of this were happening.

Rachel turned left again and drove farther into the quiet neighborhood of rock yards and chain-link fences. "You used to look at me," Rachel said. "And every time you did it behind your glasses, I knew it. I felt it."

"Are you threatening me?" Mr. Bobs asked. They drove past a Mormon church, where a man wearing a suit and tie and holding rolls of new toilet paper stacked in his arms struggled to enter the large front doors. One of the rolls toppled from the stack and sped over the sidewalk behind him. "Are you?"

"In the pictures I took of you," Rachel continued, "you've got your mouth open because you're shouting at the boys in front of you to bash their helmets together. And even though you look mad and crazy with anger, you look sad, too, because it seems like you're too angry, if you know what I mean. Angrier than a football coach should be. I've got a title," Rachel said. "It's called *The General,* or maybe *The General's Secret.* It's going to be the first photograph of the sports section." Then she said, "I'm not threatening you. I don't think I am, anyway."

"Jesus," Mr. Bobs said, laughing, though it wasn't a pleasant laugh. And when Rachel turned to look at him, he had taken his glasses off and was wiping the sweat from his forehead. "First of all, I never looked at you. Not once. And if you're planning to tell people I did, you'd better think again."

He looked exhausted, run-down, and Rachel suddenly remembered what she'd wanted to know from him. "What did it feel like," she asked, "when your wife left you? Afterward, I mean. When the house was empty. When you knew she was gone forever."

"Stop the car," Mr. Bobs said in a fierce whisper. "Stop the stupid car."

"No," Rachel said. Mr. Bobs was angry now. Thank God he was angry, furious. "We're having a driving lesson, aren't we?"

"You have two seconds to stop the car." When Rachel kept driving, Mr. Bobs slammed the brake pedal down on his side and they came to a screeching stop. He reached over and began wrestling Rachel for the keys, their hands interlocking.

"You're touching me. Stop touching me," Rachel yelled. He withdrew then, jerking back as if stung, though somehow he'd ended up with the keys.

"I'm going to give you bus money," Mr. Bobs said, digging in his pocket. "And you're going to get out right here."

"It must have hurt a lot," Rachel said. "Or maybe you didn't feel anything. Maybe you went around the house pulling all the empty drawers out, opening her closet and just looking into the space left by everything she took away, while you tried to feel something."

Mr. Bobs was holding money out to her, his hands shaking. "Get the hell out."

Rachel didn't really hate him anymore, but she had planned to hate him and she had wanted to hate him. So she said it. "You're an asshole, Mr. Bobs. You're a dirty, messy asshole." She pulled the Mace out of her front pocket, pointed it at him, and watched Mr. Bobs's face grow puzzled, then frightened.

"What?" he said.

"Bang!" she said, spraying him. He exhaled, as if all at once deflating, and folded up into his lap. Rachel felt her throat clench from the fumes and put her hand to her mouth as she looked down at his back. "Mr. Bobs," Rachel said through her hand. "Say something." He made a sound, a deep sound that did not seem human and that prompted her to touch him softly on the shoulder, where she felt his muscles quivering, where she felt what must have been his suffering. She wanted to say his first name then, to call him out of his pain with something more familiar—Robert or Earl or Dennis. But she didn't know it. She didn't know anything about this man she'd just hurt. So she said again, "Mr. Bobs. Please." He moved away from her touch and somehow let himself out of the car, dropping to the asphalt. She heard the noise of the keys he'd just snatched from her hit the ground and saw him roll over onto his back. His closed eyes streamed with tears. "Mr. Bobs," she said, now standing above him. He had begun to breathe again and she wanted to call for help, but she was too afraid of what she'd done. It was then that she noticed the children staring at her from the rock garden of the house directly in front of her. "I didn't do it," she said. They said nothing in return and she saw then that they were lawn ornaments—a little boy with a corncob pipe in his mouth and a fishing rod in his hand and a little girl with a red smile on her face, wearing a heavy winter coat and supporting a satchel of schoolbooks on her back. "Oh," she said to them. She looked at the house in front of her, a small adobe structure, and saw herself cut off at the waist and reflected in the sun-splashed glass of its single front window. No one had seen. No one had been looking. Not even a single car was driving along this road, though Rachel could hear the rushing traffic of Tucson like the sound of a river somewhere beyond the houses, the sound of the whole world, where people ate octopus, where Africans played in the dirt, where Arabs road off on camels into their strange, endless desert of sand dunes, where girls and their families picnicked on polar ice caps, the world at the quiet center of which Rachel now stood, only to see that it was dead. The world was dead. It didn't seem to care if you were a terrible person who did terrible things. It didn't seem to care about anything. It was just there, inexplicably there.

Mr. Bobs had gotten to his knees, leaned his chest against the car's front fender, fisting and unfisting one of his hands. Rachel knew she had better be gone by the time he got to his feet. She picked up Mr. Bobs's silver whistle on its yellow nylon cord—it had fallen off his neck—and put it in her pocket. This small theft seemed to count for nothing now that she had done so much worse. And when she had walked a block and turned the corner and walked three or four more blocks, she put the whistle around her neck, held it between her lips, and blew on it long and hard. She blew on it until its shrill sound ripped across the sky. She blew on it until the houses in this dead, dead neighborhood came to life a little, until a small boy stepped out of a screen door in a pair of blue flip-flops and white underwear and stared at her, until an old man appeared behind the gray glass of his living room window and touched it with his hand, as if he were captive there and wanted out, until a housewife came out on her porch smoking a cigarette and drying a serving platter with a dishrag, looking unhappy, bored, and finally unimpressed by Rachel's whistling, until a bare-chested Latino man with the word *amigo* tattooed in red letters across his chest stood up from the porch steps where he'd been sitting and gave her a military salute, and until the neighborhood dogs threw themselves against the chain-link fences of their backyards and howled because it must have hurt them to hear the long, senseless scream of her whistle. She blew on it until she grew light-headed and dark spots hovered in the air before her and she almost blacked out and fell into a soft oblivion that seemed to have opened at her shoulder, ready to receive her forever, and until, finally, she did not black out and oblivion did not swallow her and no one did anything except look, then look away, which was when she stopped, put the stupid whistle back in her pocket, and walked on.

IV

During the three-week Christmas break, Rachel waited for the police to come to her door with a warrant, or for the phone to ring, or for Father Kelsh to send a notice of her expulsion, or for Mr. Bobs himself to pound at their front door and scream out her name. But days passed and no one came, and Rachel woke in the dark mornings with a numb heart. The one time she had hurt another person, hurt him physically and without mercy, she hadn't hated him. Now she was left feeling empty and abandoned, just as she might have felt had she had sex with a boy who'd meant nothing to her. Maybe love and hate were the same in this respect. Maybe both were difficult to achieve.

Rachel's mother was surprisingly alert and well on Christmas morning. Rachel received a red Lands' End light winter coat and toothpaste, toothbrushes, Maxi hair gel, Mabeline mascara and blush, three different shades of lipstick, and, the one concession to her fading childhood, a Duncan glow-in-the-dark yo-yo that shone a milky white when they turned out the lights. Her father had done all the shopping, and the presents he gave and wrapped for himself were remarkably like the ones he'd received for years now: a necktie with red unicycles on it, a bar of Old Spice soap-on-a-rope, three boxes of Spalding Ace 1 golf balls (one of the few gifts he would actually use), and the last, a large and totally unexpected item, a "Build a ship in a bottle" kit. "I always thought ships in bottles were sort of neat and mysterious," he said. "So I thought, What the hell." The box showed an old sailing ship, the sort that Christopher Columbus and the Pilgrims had used, held inside a large corked bottle. "Mysterious," her father said again, looking at the box.

Rachel's mother opened presents last. She pulled almond Kisses and chocolate caramels from her stocking, though they all knew she had lost her appetite for sweets long ago. "Thank you," she said. She pulled out barrettes and combs for her hair, which had been growing back thickly in the months since her chemo had stopped. Rachel's father began crying very silently—the first time he'd cried openly in front of both Rachel and her mother. "Merry Christmas anyway."

He laughed as the tears came down. "Ho, ho, ho," he said,
trying to smile. Rachel's mother pulled a huge feather pillow
from a box. "Thank you," she said, putting it in her lap
and beginning to open another, which turned out to be a
square of cloth with strange attachments and a pocket in it.
"That's a phone pocket," he explained. "It attaches to the
arm of your wheelchair and you put the cordless in the
pocket. That way, the phone's always at your side." Rachel
was appalled. Her mother was not yet in a wheelchair and
these things—the pillow and the phone pocket—were
meant to help her die. Her mother just smiled. "Thank you
both," she said.

"Merry Christmas," her father said.

"Merry Christmas," Rachel heard herself say.

On New Year's Day, the doorbell rang in the middle of the
afternoon and Rachel knew it was them—the police had
come to question her, the police, with Mr. Bobs or Father
Kelsh or both. But when she looked through the peephole,
she saw Rand, his smiling face warped and pulled into a
cone by the glass. "You can't be here," she said through the
door.

"Hi," he said. "Happy New Year. Please open up."

"No."

"Please," he said, and she finally did open the door.

"You have to go," Rachel said. She felt the presence of
her mother just down the hall, dying behind the half-open
door of her bedroom. It was obscene. "I'm sorry." He
opened his mouth just as she closed the door and cut off
the desperate sound of her name—"*Rachel!*" He knocked,
then knocked again, and Rachel went around to the living
room window and watched him, tall and skinny, stare at

the front door and kick at the concrete with his tennis shoe a few times before he turned around and left.

The next day, the doorbell rang again. "I told you that you couldn't come here."

Rand began to speak rapidly in German, and the flow of that strange language on the long, sorrowful thread of Rand's voice kept her from closing the door. "I am sorry," he finally said in English.

"You can't come in," Rachel said. "But maybe I can come out." Rachel hadn't left the house for days, and she squinted in the bright light. The desert air seemed cold and raw. She had to hug her arms to keep warm, and the crumbly sidewalk stung her bare feet.

"You maybe want to put shoes on," Rand said.

"No. No I don't." She felt the sharp edge of everything then, and she liked it. Even the grass on the front lawn of the nearby church—the only grass in Rachel's neighborhood—felt individual and prickly when she sat down and leaned against her palms. Some cats came to bother them, slinking against their legs, and Rachel pushed them away.

"There is something mean about you," Rand said.

"Yep," Rachel said. "I know. So why did you come back to see me?"

Rand smiled, showing his teeth. He wore a T-shirt that said READ BOOKS in large red letters, and Rachel thought she loved him then, his intelligence, his knowledge of the world, his taste for octopus, that ugly sea creature, the large, generous smile he directed at her now, despite the fact that she was mean. "I am missing you," he said. "I am missing our English lessons. Lisa on the North Pole is asking about you. I am wondering about your pictures, your dark photographs. I miss them, too." They were silent for a while and lay on their backs and looked into the cloudless, cold sky. "My family and I are going away at the end of the summer," Rand said. "To Rio."

"I thought so," Rachel said, still looking into the simple blue sky that seemed to obliterate the drama of facing the funny, dangly-limbed, foreign boy whom she liked too much to ever let go. They were just voices speaking out of the air, and that made things easier to hear and say. "I need to tell you something," she said. "But I can't say it in my language. Would you teach me some words?"

"A German lesson?" he asked.

"Please." She asked him the word for *dying,* the word for *my,* the word—the most difficult word—for *mother.* The German was strange and seemed to break apart in her mouth, and before she could finish constructing her crumbling sentence, Rand knew.

"Oh," he said. "Oh."

"Yep," Rachel said.

"Can I help you?" Rand asked. He had sat up on the grass, and Rachel, who hadn't moved, could make out from the side of her eyes his torso slanting hugely above her, taking up half the sky. She had to look away.

"I don't think so," she said.

When school started again in January, something seemed different, though Rachel could not guess what it was. The shabby brown halls lined with gray padlocked lockers seemed unchanged. The stink of shoe leather and pencil erasure was the same. Perhaps her classmates had grown taller and more greasy-faced; teenagers were always growing and sprouting pimples, and Rachel herself felt a new and painful constellation of zits coming in above her nose.

And her bra had become snug; its little hook bit into her soft back, and somehow she would soon have to ask her grieving father to buy her the next size up. How would she even begin to mention her growing breasts to him?

She and Rand spent more and more time together, though they no longer kissed, really. They sometimes cuddled on Rand's bed and gave each other brief squeezes and hugs. But they did not approach the terrors of first sex again. Rachel continued to enhance his vocabulary. And on Ash Wednesday, after the school Mass, Rand approached her, looking perplexed. He, like Rachel and all of the students at Our Lady, wore a cross of ashes—black charcoal—on his forehead, like a burn mark that signified a commitment to sacrifice and a Christ-like life. During the Mass, nuns and priests stationed at the end of each pew had dipped their fingers in a pot of black dust and marked the foreheads of students as they proceeded to the altar to receive Communion. It was silly, Rachel thought, all these teenagers pretending to be disciples of the Son of God. "What is the meaning of the word *retribution*?" he asked her.

This word felt like a slap in the face to Rachel. She thought she'd been listening closely to Father Kelsh's reflection on the Gospel that afternoon, but she had not heard him say *retribution* and she could not fight off the feeling that Rand's ignorance was now trying to teach her something. "It means that God is punishing," she said. "It means 'payback.' "

"God is cruel," he said without much conviction.

"No," Rachel said. "God is sleeping."

Rachel would pass Mr. Bobs in the hallway now and then, but he would conspicuously—with a certain extravagance—pretend not to notice her, and this treatment made her feel smaller, diminished in the world. He wore a new whistle around his neck, as if she had never humiliated him and stolen from him.

Rachel's duties as a photographer continued, though as January moved into February, she noticed that her work had settled into the sort of peaceful cliché that Mr. Marcosian had wanted. She showed the girl's basketball team carrying Katie Lopez on their shoulders after their victory over Sonora High. She showed Marcus Ray goose-stepping and holding aloft the pigskin in the end zone after a touchdown. Then, during the football state championship game in February, Rat Swank failed to rise from a pileup and Rachel raced down to the sidelines, where she saw him, his fat linebacker's gut spilling white and fleshy from his jersey and his face splattered with new, undried blood. She aimed her camera just as Mr. Bobs put his hand up in front of her lens and said, "For heaven's sake, girl!" in a tone of utter disgust that left her stunned. She put the camera down and watched as Coach Bobs and two other coaches attended to the injured player. "How many fingers am I holding up, son?" Mr. Bobs was asking softly. He held the back of Rat's bloody head in one hand and put out three fingers with the other. "How many?"

"It doesn't hurt. Not at all," Rat said. He had that look in his eyes that she had seen first in the driver's ed movies, that look as if he saw beyond what Father Mannon, Rachel's religion teacher that term, called "the veil," and Rachel was afraid for him. Who knew what the poor, injured fat boy saw then. A bright light? A bottomless darkness? And what had he done to anybody? Just the week before, Rachel had written the worst homosexual message about him on the bathroom stall divider. "Billy Bat bones Rat Swank up his

mousy butt." All those *b*'s had been so compelling to pronounce that she'd read it out loud again and again to herself
as she dried the stupid tears from her eyes.

Thank God he recovered from his minor concussion and
could be seen three days later walking through the halls of
Our Lady without so much as a bandage, looking as dull-
eyed and physically massive as ever.

Then, in early March, on a Wednesday afternoon, the
sleeping world began to wake and push back at Rachel. Just
after she'd finished crying in the basement bathroom, someone walked in and stood in front of her stall. "Who's in
there?" this person asked. In the strange, cavernous acous-
tics of the bathroom, the voice speaking from the other side
of the stall took on a God-like depth and solidity.

"No one," Rachel said back. She had pulled her feet up
onto the toilet seat and was hugging her knees, trembling and
looking down between her feet at the pool of toilet water,
where she saw the icy edges of her own reflection. "Go away,"
she said, though she somehow dropped her black felt-tipped
marker then and watched it hit the tiles and roll out beneath
the stall door into plain sight. A fist hammered on the stall
door. "Open up this minute!" She obeyed and found herself
looking up at Sister Mariam Anne's chalky old face framed in
a baby blue habit. She held up the evidence of the black
marker in a fist. "Evil girl," the nun said, looking away from
Rachel's partial nakedness. "Fasten your pants, little lady.
Fasten them this minute."

Up the two flights of stairs on the way to Father Kelsh's
office, Sister Mariam Anne held Rachel at arm's length,
gripping her earlobe and twisting it until Rachel hunched
over and felt that side of her head blaze with a pain that
shivered into her right arm and made her eyes fill with
tears. "Evil girl," Sister Mariam Anne said again as she

stood her before Father Kelsh, who sat calmly at his desk, as if he'd been waiting hours for this moment. Behind Father Kelsh stood a huge glass case filled with the gilded trophies of the school's athletic state titles, trophies nearly as tall as Rachel herself. She cried out loud and choked a little on the strong aerosol odor of the old nun.

"What is the problem, Sister?" Father Kelsh asked.

"This little lady," she said, "is our graffiti *artist*, Father." She came down especially hard on the word *artist,* and Rachel understood now that she had been stalked, hunted, and captured. She was the *graffiti artist*. She was at the middle of a drama of justice and punishment.

"Oh," he said. "You can sit down, Rachel." His voice lacked severity, which seemed to disappoint Sister Mariam Anne.

"She's the one," the old lady said.

"Thank you, Sister." His eyes told her to leave the room, and she did. "So," Father Kelsh asked, "did you write the graffiti?"

"No," Rachel said. But then she changed her mind. "Yes. I did it."

"Thank you for the truth," he said. Father Kelsh's slightly chubby face remained calm. "You upset people, you know. You used real names, names of students and teachers at Our Lady. Can you tell me why?"

"I don't think I can," Rachel said.

Father Kelsh smoothed down his plump mustache, thought for a moment, and then seemed to accept Rachel's silence. "You will stop now, won't you?" She nodded her head. Then he said it outright, without any anger in his voice. "We will have to suspend you for a few days." None of this was the way she'd imagined it over and over again when she'd seen Father Kelsh and Mr. Bobs waiting for her with the police at the front door. Where were the biblical curses, the black accusations, the fierce voices? In his Masses, Father Kelsh evidently spoke of retribution. But here, in his office, he was just a person who seemed a little shy and hesitant over the phone when he said to her father, "We need to ask you to come pick up Rachel." In less than ten minutes, her father showed up in his work suit and the red unicycle tie, which Father Kelsh actually complimented in passing. "Thank you," her father said. "It was a Christmas present from my wife." And this small, strikingly false statement would be what Rachel would remember most about that day. What bullshit. What terrible bullshit. Her mother, her father's wife, was a dying woman, a woman who could give them nothing now, not even a tacky, stupid necktie.

In the car, her father tried and failed to be a disciplinarian. "I'm not exactly sure what to do about this," he said. "But I don't think we should tell your mother."

"Okay. Sure. Let's not tell her." Then she said, "You lied to Father Kelsh."

"I did?"

"Mom didn't give you that tie. You gave that tie to yourself."

Her father glanced at her, then watched the road again. "There's something a little nasty about you right now, a little hurtful."

She seemed to be demanding this sincerity from people lately, first from Rand and now from her father. "I know it," she said. Then she made what she hoped would be a confession. "I lie, too. I lie all the time." To her surprise, her father let this go. He just drove on in silence and left Rachel alone with her secrets and her lies.

During the few days of her suspension, Rachel watched her father, who'd get off work at noon, then spend long hours gluing his wooden ship together on a card table in the basement. How did a ship get into a bottle? It was just as everyone suspected. The bottom of the bottle was the last piece to be glued on.

On the same card table, her father had set up a small white speaker, in which they could hear the sound—a little bit like a wind or the risings and swellings of the sea—of her mother breathing upstairs in her room. Rachel half-expected it to stop at any time—the sea, the wind of her mother's life. But it didn't. Not yet. From time to time, they'd hear her rouse, painfully swallow or even moan, then fall back into that constant rhythm.

One afternoon, Rachel went downstairs to an empty basement and looked at the stupid white speaker as she listened to the voices of her parents speaking to each other. "I worry about you and Rachel," her mother said.

"There's nothing to worry about," her father said.

"I hate to picture it—you two alone in the evenings. The father and the daughter at the dinner table. The father and the daughter without the mother. It seems terribly lonely."

"Not at all," he said. "I mean, it will be lonely. But Rachel and I will manage."

"How?" she asked. "What will you do?"

"Please," he said. "I'd rather not talk about this. Not now."

And because Rachel could no longer stand to hear about it, she walked out of the room.

"I learned about that part of history last year," she told her father one afternoon in the basement as he delicately sheathed the small cloth sails to the booms of his model ship.

"What?" he said.

"Christopher Columbus. The *Niña,* the *Santa María,* and the *Pinta,*" Rachel said.

"Falling off the edge of the world."

"Yeah," Rachel said. "But the real problem for them was scurvy. When they ran out of citrus fruit. No vitamin C. People got sores and scabs. They lost their hair, their fingernails. Their flesh just sort of fell apart. They'd kill one another for a wedge of lemon to suck on. But all they had was salted meat, and that didn't help." She remembered now how much pleasure Mr. Marcosian, her history teacher last year, had taken in describing the sort of deterioration Columbus's crew had suffered. As much as he disliked her photographs, Mr. Marcosian had an appetite for darkness, imagining the worst. Everybody did, it seemed.

"That's not the sort of voyage I picture," her father said. "Blue seas, winds that ripple the water, the smell of sea air, dolphins at the bow."

"That's not true," she said. "It's not like that." She thought of the North Pole—no bears, no penguins, nothing but whiteness, empty whiteness.

"Maybe it's a little bit like that."

Rachel didn't know. She had never seen the sea, save for on TV, where it was usually portrayed as a villain, harboring terrible man-eating sharks and spewing storms at innocent people. That couldn't be true, either. "Maybe," she said. "What will we do without her?" Rachel asked then.

"What?"

"After Mom dies," Rachel said, "what will you and I do?"

"Oh," he said, still focusing entirely on the ship.

She just said it then. "I need new bras. I'm growing, I guess."

Her father flubbed it and let the mainsail fall. "Really?" he said, actually looking at her.

"Please don't stare," she said.

He looked away. "How will we do that?"

"Maybe you could drive me to the mall and give me some money. You don't have to come in or anything."

"Sure," he said. "That sounds like a plan."

And it seemed to Rachel then that she and her father would figure out how to be survivors, how to be stranded and left behind together. "It's a plan," Rachel said.

It was true. Rachel openly admitted it. She was mean. But it was also true that this meanness had been leaving her for some time now, seeping away a little bit every day as fall became winter, as the relentless light turned white and cold and more distant, as the rain of a Sonoran spring returned and the days grew long and, a few weeks later, the sky became a vacuous hot sheet of blue in which the sun turned on again, bristled, beat down on everything, and made the air warp and bend. The meanness was leaving her and she felt its gradual departure. Just as everything else left, just as everything else was only temporary, so was her hurtfulness. When the saleslady with large hair and drawn eyebrows who sold her three blouses at Nordstrom winked at her and her father and said, "It's sweet to see a man shopping with his daughter. We don't get that often," Rachel felt a little bit of the meanness falling away. When Rachel said carefully at the dinner table at Rand's house, *"Diese Kartoffeln schmecken gut!"* which meant "These potatoes taste good" (and they did taste good), and Rand and his parents applauded her for her pronunciation, she felt a little bit more of it go. Even when the director of the hospice where her mother would soon go to die, a woman who wore round wire spectacles and had close-cropped hair like ruffled feathers, said, "Our central belief here is that death is part of life, that families and their loved ones should be made as comfortable as possible in a comfortable, natural setting," to which Rachel thought, What do you know, you bitch? even then Rachel knew her meanness would leave, would go finally.

In the late spring, Mr. Marcosian allowed Rachel to place her two favorite photographs in the yearbook—the portrait of a fierce Mr. Bobs and the picture of the toppled cheerleaders called *The Agony and the Ecstasy: Girls Feel Pain, Too!* He reluctantly agreed with Rachel that this work's title had a feminist ring, even if the photograph itself showed a strange choreography of prostrated girls. No one, it was true, much liked her darker work. But it seemed to Rachel that suffering was more real, indisputably real, than anything else, so real that you had to tell people lies about your necktie, you had to mark up the walls with insults, you had to vandalize the yearbook's sports section with the shadows of loss and pain. You had to reach out and hate someone, or at least try to hate someone. You had to.

Before school let out for the summer, Rachel did one last thing. She cut out five words from a magazine article and glued them to an index card, as if she were a blackmailer, a kidnapper, an extortionist, to construct the sentence "I am very very sorry," then put it together with Mr. Bobs's stolen whistle in a manila envelope, which she sealed and left outside his office door. She felt it then, too, a little bit more of her meanness going.

She didn't know why she spent so much time with Rand

now that he would be leaving in a few weeks, and she told him so. "It just makes things worse," she said.

He promised to write, to E-mail often. He said, "You can just know that I am out there. That's a good thing to know."

"Out there," Rachel said, trying to feel better. She thought of Rand in a jar, the rain coming down, the old ladies and Mrs. Taub weeping and weeping. No flowers, not even one. She wept, too. For the first time in she couldn't remember how long, she cried openly. Rand looked a little scared. He was just a boy, after all. "Don't worry," she said. "I'll stop soon." And she did.

In the afternoons, Rachel sat at her mother's bedside, wearing one of her new blouses from Nordstrom and a little lipstick, though her mother was too tired to notice now and wore no makeup herself, her illness finally having overcome her vanity. Now and then, she would wake and sit up in bed and stare at the bad painting of the little boat on the wall across from her and make simple conversation. "Tell me about the weather. How is your father? How is school? Tell me about your German boy." Rachel would give her simple answers and watch her mother's large eyes, which seemed less and less able to rise out of sleep, which seemed now to reflect a world submerged in pain and darkness. Where are you going? Rachel wanted to ask her, but she didn't. Are you scared? How much does it hurt? Instead, she said, "Dad has finished constructing his ship. He's painting it now very slowly. You know what a perfectionist he is." She half-expected her quiet mother to ask her again at any moment that terrible question about the deserted island, that stupid boat that her mother kept staring at. And though she never did ask it, Rachel had settled on an answer. She'd decided that she would not wish to go to that island, that she would not submit to that strange fantasy's conditions, its horrible limits—What three things would you take?—and if she were forced to submit and placed in that simple white boat that her dead grandmother had painted and asked that question, she would answer in defiance, "Nothing. Nothing. I'll take nothing."